THE HU

The people of the Clan have always lived peacefully on the Slopes overlooking the Greenlands, hunting only for food and respecting the Greenlands' unwritten laws. But when the Clan's cattle become the prey of an unknown attacker, a young chief blames the Feln – huge catlike animals – and orders their extermination.

Because of his refusal to kill a Feln, the boy Tal is forced to live a life of drudgery, despised by the other members of the Clan. But he escapes and sets out on a perilous journey to find help for the Clan against the evil that truly threatens them.

A masterly novel of adventure and fantasy by the author of *Forbidden Paths of Thual* and *Master of the Grove* (both published in Puffin).

VICTOR KELLEHER

THE HUNTING OF SHADROTH

PUFFIN BOOKS

Puffin Books, Penguin Books Ltd, Harmondsworth, Middlesex, England
Viking Penguin Inc., 40 West 23rd Street, New York, New York 10010, U.S.A.
Penguin Books Australia Ltd, Ringwood, Victoria, Australia
Penguin Books Canada Ltd, 2801 John Street, Markham, Ontario, Canada L3R 1B4
Penguin Books (N.Z.) Ltd, 182–190 Wairau Road, Auckland 10, New Zealand

First published by Kestrel Books 1981
Published in Puffin Books 1983
Reprinted 1985

Made and printed in Great Britain by
Richard Clay (The Chaucer Press) Ltd, Bungay, Suffolk
Set in Ehrhardt

Contents

PART I · THE MENACE

1. Look-out

Tal was sitting on a rocky outcrop at the very edge of the hillside. Behind him, but some distance away, were the cave dwellings where he had lived all his life – rooms and passageways which had been hollowed out of the sheer rock face of the cliff long before he was born. Nearer at hand, the cattle belonging to the Clan grazed peacefully in the afternoon sunlight, cropping the grass which grew on the gentle slope immediately below him. At the bottom of this long slope the vast Greenlands began, filling the whole of the huge plain and stretching far away into the distance to where the hazy outline of the mountains showed against the sky.

From time to time Tal would glance up, his eyes narrowed against the glare, and stare out over the miles of lush greenery. Although still a boy, he was practised in reading and interpreting the signs of the Greenlands. The call or the flight of birds, the slightest movement of the tiny squirrel-tailed apes in the tree-tops, were enough to put him on the alert. But now, in the heat of the day, nothing stirred. And after a few moments of watchfulness he returned to the task at which he had been busy most of the day.

He was painting a picture on a large square piece of dried bark, and it was clear from the expression on his face that something was puzzling him. What he had painted so far showed a scene somewhere in the Greenlands: tall vine-covered trees towering over a grassy clearing; around the edge of this clearing a circle of men, all armed with a star-knife or sling; and at the centre of the circle, one of the Feln. The Feln were great cats, many times the size of a man, which roamed throughout the dense growth of the Greenlands. This one was not standing still like the armed hunters who surrounded it.

Instead, it was shown in the act of charging straight ahead, fangs bared, as though trying to burst its way out of the painting in order to attack Tal himself.

This in itself was puzzling enough: Feln had never been known to attack a human – never, in all the history of the Clan. Yet for some reason that he couldn't understand, Tal had felt compelled to paint the Feln in this way: charging straight towards him, its yellow eyes glinting, its fangs ready to tear at his throat. Nor was this the only puzzling thing in the picture. Behind the charging Feln was an empty space, in which he had painted nothing. Several times he had tried to fill it in, but had been unable to. He knew that something must go there; something enormous, brooding, a threatening presence watching from the undergrowth. Repeatedly he made himself concentrate to the point where he could almost see it lurking there, dangerous, a vague outline of darkness; but the moment he picked up his brush, the vision would dissolve and he would find himself again staring at the empty space. Try as he might, he could not make the shape come clear in his mind. It was exactly as if some alien creature were hiding behind the foliage he had painted, biding its time, refusing to show itself until it was ready.

With a gesture of frustration Tal laid aside his brush – and was immediately startled by the sound of a light step right behind him. He turned quickly and found himself staring into the dark eyes of Kulok, the young newly appointed leader of the Clan.

As always since his return from the Greenlands, Kulok was wearing the cloak made from the tawny yellow skin of a Feln. Beneath the cloak he was naked except for a loin-cloth and a strange black charm that hung from a cord around his neck. The charm, too, he had brought back with him from the Greenlands: dull and oddly shapeless, it seemed almost to absorb the light, and was more like a deep shadow on the young chieftain's chest than a hard tangible object.

As though sensing Tal's interest in the charm, Kulok drew the cloak tightly about him and gazed sternly at the boy.

8

'You are supposed to be on look-out,' he said angrily. 'Is this the way you fulfil your duty to the Clan?'

Tal felt his face reddening.

'The Greenlands are quiet now,' he began to explain, 'there is no sign of . . .'

'Do you imagine the Feln would announce their arrival?' Kulok interrupted him scornfully. 'They are masters of silence. It is at just such a time as this, when you would least expect danger, that they are most likely to strike.'

Tal lowered his eyes, remembering his grandfather's advice and forcing himself to remain silent.

'Even now,' Kulok went on, 'they might be watching us from the edge of the Greenlands.'

'The Feln do not attack the people of the Clan,' Tal murmured softly.

'That is a tale fit only for the old and for dreamers,' Kulok answered quickly. 'Haven't I faced the Feln alone and understood their true nature? How do you think I came by this?'

He held out the edge of his cloak, trying to make Tal finger the smooth yellow fur, but the boy drew back nervously.

'Are you like the old people up there?' Kulok asked. 'Do you fear even to touch it? Do you think that I alone acted aggressively in obtaining it – that the Feln was not also to blame?'

Tal again lowered his eyes.

'I could never wear such a thing,' he said quietly.

He expected another angry reply, but Kulok merely placed one hand gently on his shoulder.

'Be reasonable, Tal,' he said. 'We have all been taught the old tales. It would be pleasant to go on believing in them. But how can we? You know as well as I that the cattle have been disturbed for some nights past. And what else is there, between here and the far mountains, large and powerful enough to frighten them? It can only be the Feln. There is no other explanation.'

'The Feln would not worry the cattle on the Slopes,' Tal said stubbornly. 'It is not their domain.'

'Then who or what is worrying them?'

Tal shrugged helplessly.

'I don't know,' he admitted.

'In that case,' Kulok said, his voice growing stern once again, 'I would advise you to give more attention to your duty. You were put on look-out because you have the sharpest eyes of anybody in the Clan. Despite your youth, there is nobody who can read the Greenlands as you can. Where others see nothing, you will see a sign. Even the rustling of the leaves in the trees has words for you. Therefore use your talent well. Watch carefully and put aside these games.'

He indicated the square of bark on Tal's lap – and as he did so, he seemed to notice for the first time what the painting represented. Instantly, he looked sharply at Tal.

'Are you playing with me, boy?' he asked impatiently.

Tal glanced up, surprised.

'Playing . . .?'

Kulok pointed at the picture.

'You tell me the Feln are peaceful. And at the same time you show them as savage and dangerous. How do you explain such a contradiction?'

Tal hesitated before replying.

'I cannot explain it,' he said. 'I have never thought of the Feln in this way; but for some reason this is how the painting came out.'

Kulok fingered his soft beard thoughtfully.

'Could it be that you have the Gift?' he said, speaking as much to himself as to Tal.

'My grandfather, Nator, thinks it is possible,' Tal replied.

'And you,' Kulok asked, 'what do you think?'

'I'm not sure. Nator says we must be patient and wait. The Gift is something which increases with the years.'

'Just the same,' Kulok murmured, 'it is a possibility worth considering.'

And he leaned forward and inspected the painting more closely.

With Kulok leaning over him like that, Tal did not dare move for fear of touching the border of the Feln-skin cloak. He remained quite still, his eyes only a matter of inches from the black charm which hung from Kulok's neck. He had not been so close to it before. As it swung slowly to and fro, its shape seemed to shift and change, never still. The only constant thing about it, which he had not noticed until now, was two tiny red dots near the top.

He was actually on the point of asking about the charm when Kulok pointed to the empty space in the painting.

'What do you intend putting here?' he asked.

'I . . . I . . . haven't yet decided,' Tal stammered out – unwilling to explain the strange thoughts he had had about that space.

But even as he spoke, his attention was distracted once again by the black charm. And he suddenly understood with a peculiar feeling of shock that the charm itself was what he had been searching for. It was, in some disturbing sense, the dark presence which watched from the cover of the painted undergrowth.

To his relief, at that very moment of insight Kulok straightened up and put the charm beyond his reach.

'I should like to see this painting when it is finished,' he said. 'You must bring it to my cavern. But now, as I have already told you, your task is to watch. You are the eyes and ears of the Clan while you stand guard here. Perform your duty well.'

Without waiting for a reply Kulok strode away towards the dwellings. Tal watched him go, sitting quietly only until he was sure Kulok was no longer spying on him. Then he selected one of the small earthenware pots carefully laid out on a level slab of rock near by. This particular pot contained a black pigment which he tested on the smooth skin of his palm. Unsatisfied with its quality, he added to it a few pinches of the dark gritty soil which had collected in a crack in the rock on which he sat. Now the pigment was more to his liking: a dead, dull black, showing no trace of grey. And moistening it with his spittle, he blacked out the remaining space in the painting.

He had also intended to paint in the tiny red dots which he had noticed on the charm, but the effect of the black, squat shape, lodged there at the edge of the clearing, waiting, was somehow so realistic and threatening that he postponed finishing the painting and hastily put it aside, leaving it face down on the rock beside him. Even so, he continued to feel oddly disturbed, and it cost him an effort to put all thought of the painting out of his mind.

Now, with his attention at last fixed on the task of watching, he was slightly surprised to discover how late it was. Down on the broad plain, the worst heat of the day had already passed and the whole of the Greenlands was slowly coming to life. The tops of the trees stirred lazily in the late afternoon breeze, the broad shiny leaves of vines glinting in the yellowish light. Birds, singly and in small flocks, went skimming colourfully between the branches.

In all this growing activity, there was nothing to alarm him or arouse his suspicion. It was a scene as familiar to him as his own hands. Nonetheless, he remained on the alert now, listening to the bird calls, his eyes attracted instantly by the slightest movement.

Still nothing disturbed the familiar scene. Slowly the sun began to drop lower in the sky, and over towards the west the snow-covered tops of the mountains flashed gold, their upper slopes changing from mauve to black as they were plunged into shadow. Normally that line of dark shadow, so far distant that it could not be seen clearly, had no sinister quality about it. It was nothing more than the first sign of encroaching night. But on this particular occasion it had an unusual effect on Tal. He found that he was unable to tear his eyes away from it. In vain he listened for some recognizable sound of distress or alarm from the Greenlands below him. All, it seemed, was calm and peaceful; not so much as a single bird echoed his own vague uneasiness. Yet still that uneasiness persisted, like a nagging doubt somewhere in the back of his mind.

He remembered what Kulok had said earlier: how he could perceive a sign where others saw nothing. Was this disturbed feeling therefore a sign? And if so, of what? He could give no clear answer to these questions. He merely knew, almost with a sixth sense, that something was wrong: something had changed in this scene that he had grown to know so well. That something, whatever it might be, was presently situated on the far side of the plain – hidden by the slowly advancing line of shadow; and, like that shadow, coming steadily closer.

2. The Presence

For the second time that day Tal was startled by the sound of footsteps. Momentarily distracted, he turned and saw Lea, Kulok's sister, walking across the rocks towards him. She was much younger than her brother, almost the same age as Tal. As far back as he could remember, they had always been good friends; but since the death of her father, the old chieftain, they had grown even closer – partly, perhaps, because they were both orphans and understood each other better for that reason.

'I would have come earlier,' she said, 'but you know what Kulok's like. He insisted that nobody should disturb you while you were on look-out, so I had to wait until he was busy. As if there was anything to worry . . .'

She suddenly stopped, noticing the baffled expression on Tal's face.

'What's troubling you?' she asked, her voice dropping almost to a whisper.

'I'm not sure,' he said, his forehead still furrowed with concentration.

She stood close beside him and he pointed into the far distance.

'It's over there,' he said, 'in the foothills of the mountains.'

'I can see only the evening shadow,' she said softly.

He nodded.

'Yes, that – but something else too.'

By now the advancing shadow had reached the far edge of the Greenlands and was beginning to move slowly across the plain.

'We should find out something more quite soon,' he murmured.

They waited patiently for several minutes, and then, faintly at first, they detected a distant clamour of bird calls and the cries of other wild creatures. The unusual noise grew steadily louder and nearer, like a message being passed rapidly through the tree-tops.

Lea shook her head in bewilderment.

'What does it mean?' she said.

Tal listened for a few moments longer.

'It's the sound of fear,' he said quietly. 'There's some menace moving within the evening shadow. The birds are telling everything to flee towards the sunlight. Look, see for yourself.'

Sure enough, there was an abnormal amount of movement in the Greenlands as hundreds, perhaps thousands, of living creatures hurried eastwards, towards where Tal and Lea were standing.

'Will they come up here, onto the Slopes?' Lea asked uncertainly.

Tal shook his head.

'I don't think so. See, they are already gathering at the very edge of the Greenlands. They dare not leave the cover of the thick undergrowth. Up here on the Slopes they would be easy prey.'

'Yes, but a prey to what?' Lea asked. 'What exactly are they trying to escape from?'

'There's only one way to find that out,' Tal answered.

And, together, he and Lea jumped from the rocky outcrop and ran down the hillside towards the thick green wall of tangled vines and leafy branches.

In that easterly part of the plain the sun was still visible above the far mountains, its yellow rays slanting down into the thick cover of vegetation. Within this sun-speckled undergrowth Tal and Lea were amazed at the abundance of wildlife which swarmed all around them. Rain birds, brightly coloured parrots and troops of tiny apes flitted through the branches above their heads, while at ground level there were scores of animals – antelopes, porcupines, even a few fiercely tusked wild pigs.

Moving as quietly as possible in an attempt not to add to the general atmosphere of alarm, the two children forced their way through the heavy foliage towards a near-by clearing. But just before they reached it, they were stopped in their tracks: for there, standing alone in the open space, was one of the Feln. She was a magnificent female, her smooth glossy coat and brilliant eyes as yellow as the sunlight itself. At that moment she was pacing nervously to and fro. She would move in the direction of the Slopes, suddenly scent the breeze, and instantly cringe away from the smell of man. Then she would turn back towards the west, pause and flatten her ears as she snarled in fear and anger.

It was perfectly clear to both children that she was caught between two opposing forces: man on the one hand, and whatever unknown threat was advancing towards her in the evening shadow. But why did she fear man, Tal asked himself, what had any of the Clan ever done . . .? Abruptly, he understood. He was about to whisper his discovery to Lea, but already she had turned to him with a question of her own.

'Why is the Feln alone?' she asked him softly. 'I thought they mated for life and usually moved in pairs.'

Tal leaned over and put his lips close to Lea's ear.

'Her mate has probably been killed,' he said. 'Kulok now wears his skin as a cloak.'

At the sound of a human voice, the Feln whirled around and stared directly at where they were hidden, her fangs bared in a snarl of suspicion. For a second or two she seemed poised between flight and attack. And Tal, gripped by fear in spite of all that he had said earlier to Kulok, began to edge slowly away. But before he could take more than a few shuffling steps, Lea reached out and squeezed his arm, while with her other hand she motioned for him to remain silent. That quiet display of courage steadied him, and together they held their ground and waited.

The Feln, meanwhile, had also given up all thought of flight. With her whole massive body tensed for action, she inched forward across the clearing and finally thrust her head through the foliage which hid them from view.

Neither of the children had ever been so close to a Feln before, and the sheer size of the head, which was now barely more than an arm's length away, made them flinch back. Tal could feel prickles of sweat breaking out on his scalp; and Lea's grip on his arm was so tight that it was almost painful.

The Feln looked first at Lea, as though storing this strange human image up in her memory. Then, deliberately, she turned towards Tal. He drew in his breath, bracing himself to meet the challenge of those great yellow eyes; but to his amazement they presented him with no real challenge at all. There was no hatred or savagery visible in their depths, nor any distrust or fear: there was merely a calm look of recognition.

Tal was never quite certain how long he and the Feln remained silently staring into each other's eyes. Vaguely, somewhere in the background, he heard Lea say:

'Tal, what is it?'

But it wasn't that which distracted him. Rather, it was the gradual darkening of the Greenlands all around them as the sun finally dropped behind the western mountains.

All at once the stir of life at the edge of the Greenlands ceased. The cries of panic and of warning were stilled and there was no longer the slightest suggestion of movement anywhere. Even the gentle evening breeze seemed to have dropped.

Tal strained his ears, trying to detect the faintest noise of anything moving towards them; but no sound disturbed the abrupt silence. He looked quizzically at Lea . . . and at that instant it arrived. Not a physical presence, but a sudden change in the atmosphere: like a gust of ice-cold air, so cold that it clutched at their throats and lungs, making it difficult for them to breathe.

With a flick of the tail the Feln turned and was gone, disappearing into the darkness which was rapidly deepening around them.

'What's happening?' Lea whispered in a frightened voice.

Tal quickly signalled for her not to speak, and pointed in the direction they had come from.

Hand in hand, and without another word, they hurried back as quickly as the tangle of vines and bushes would allow. On every side they could make out the shadowy outlines of small animals frozen into immobility by fear or bewilderment or by the simple realization that no other refuge was left to them now.

16

To the confused and frightened minds of Tal and Lea, it appeared that they were the only living beings left – as though the icy hand of death had touched and stilled that part of the Greenlands – and despite the searing cold which threatened to stifle them, they hurried even faster, clawing at the matted undergrowth which barred their way.

When at last they broke out onto the grassy slope it was almost completely dark – unnaturally so for that time of the evening. Now that they were clear of the trees, the atmosphere had become noticeably warmer; but still they didn't stop, running and stumbling up the slope to the rocky outcrop where, thankfully, there was no trace of the icy coldness.

'Have you any idea of what happened down there?' Lea asked uncertainly.

They were standing with their arms around each other, for both warmth and reassurance. Tal shivered briefly, not only from the cold.

'Whatever it was,' he said, 'it seems to have stopped advancing. Like the animals, it obviously doesn't want to come out onto . . .'

He was interrupted by a lowing cry of pain and terror. It came from the slope somewhere along to their right and was unmistakably made by one of the cattle. Already the other cattle were galloping across the hillside in panic, their milk-white bodies flashing past in the gloom. Only seconds later men began running down from the cave dwellings, flaming torches held high above their heads.

Tal and Lea followed the line of torches to where the cow had cried out in agony. There was no sign of the poor animal now. All that remained was a splash of fresh blood on the grass and a clear indication that a heavy bleeding body had been dragged down the slope. While they were still looking at these distressing signs, Kulok hurried into the circle of light. He glanced briefly at the bloody trail, and then across at Tal.

'You were supposed to be on guard,' he said accusingly. 'Why did you sound no warning?'

'I didn't think that this . . . that this . . .' he began, and stopped.

He was still feeling shocked by what had taken place and couldn't find the right words.

'Were there no indications of danger?' Kulok asked.

'Yes,' he stammered out haltingly, 'there were signs.'

'Then why didn't you give the alarm?'

'You don't understand,' Lea broke in.

But Kulok pushed her roughly to one side.

'Be silent!' he commanded.

He turned back to Tal, his young strong-boned face suddenly calm.

'You admit there were indications of danger,' he said quietly. 'Are you telling me that you knew the Feln was down there?'

'That isn't what I meant,' Tal said desperately.

'Never mind what you meant,' Kulok countered, 'just answer my questions. Was the Feln there?'

'Yes, it was, but . . .'

'Nor am I interested in your buts,' Kulok cut in. 'It's too late for excuses now.'

'They aren't just excuses,' Lea said. 'I was there.'

Kulok pointedly ignored her.

'You are the one who was on guard, Tal,' he said, 'and so it is for you alone to answer me. Do you understand that?'

Tal nodded miserably.

'Very well then. You claim that the Feln was there; and yet you didn't warn anybody. Why is that?'

Tal took a deep breath and tried to make himself keep calm.

'I've never really believed that the Feln are what we have to fear,' he said slowly. 'I'm sure of that now.'

'Can you seriously stand there and tell me such a thing while this blood is still fresh upon the ground?' Kulok asked incredulously. 'Have you gone mad? Don't you trust the evidence of your eyes any longer?'

'This is not the only evidence,' Tal replied.

'Go on, explain yourself.'

'There is something else in the Greenlands, apart from the Feln. I went down there and felt it – a presence.'

Again he paused, struggling to find the right words, but Kulok had already held up his hand for silence.

'Did you actually leave your post and enter the Greenlands?'

'Yes.'

The young chieftain shook his head in disbelief.

'I see this is more serious than I thought,' he said. 'I give you one hour to prepare your defence. Then you must answer not only to me, but to the full Council.'

With a gesture of dismissal, Kulok pushed past him and strode off into the darkness.

3. The Gift

Tal's grandfather, Nator, was waiting for him just within the entrance of the cave dwelling. Even in the dim light of the rush lamp his old face appeared strained and anxious.

'Kulok has been here,' he said. 'He is going to all the members of the Council. Is it true what he says?'

'Part of it is true,' Tal answered wearily. 'One of the cattle has been slaughtered.'

'And the Feln?' Nator asked.

'Yes, I have seen one of the Feln, but she is not the culprit.'

'Then what is?'

'I don't know. That is what I have less than an hour to work out.'

Tal went to the back of the cave and filled a bowl with sour milk from the closed pot which always stood in the corner. He took a long drink and wiped his mouth thoughtfully.

'Grandfather,' he said at last, 'you are one of the oldest members of the Clan; you know as much about the life of the Greenlands as any person living. Apart from the Feln, is there anything out there that could kill and carry off a fully grown cow?'

The old man paced uneasily across the cave and sat down.

'There are stories and ancient legends,' he said, waving one hand vaguely in the air. 'But they would be of no help to you before the Council.'

'Can't you tell me some of them just the same?' Tal pleaded.

Nator shook his head doubtfully.

'This is not the time to speak of such things,' he said.'What we must do now is decide what you are to tell the Council.'

'But don't you see,' Tal answered, 'there's really nothing to decide. I can only tell them what little I know – that there is some other power or presence in the Greenlands.'

Nator looked at him sharply.

'Another presence, you say?'

'Yes.'

'Can you describe it?'

'No, that's why I need to find out about the ancient legends. They might be of some help.'

Still the old man hesitated. He sat with eyes cast down, refusing to look at his young grandson.

'At least tell me about my parents,' Tal added. 'I know only that they died somewhere in the Greenlands. What exactly happened to them? Surely I'm old enough to be told the truth.'

Nator sighed and looked up.

'Yes,' he said reluctantly, 'you deserve to know that at least.' There was a long pause while he collected his thoughts. 'You have probably heard already of Argalna, who was one of the greatest hunters in the history of the Clan. He and Norn, your father, were close friends and always hunted in the Greenlands together. Always, that is, except for one occasion. There was some argument which I never understood, and he and Norn went out separately. Norn didn't return alive. That was soon after you were born. Your mother had also entered the Greenlands and she, too, was never seen alive again.'

'But how did they meet their deaths?'

'That is difficult to say,' Nator went on. 'It was Argalna himself who eventually found their bodies – far across the plain near the Broad River.'

'Didn't they have any wounds?' Tal asked. 'Wasn't it clear what had killed them?'

'No, there was nothing that you could call a wound.' Nator rubbed his hands across his eyes, still obviously distressed by the memory. 'The only thing about them that had changed was the bare skin of their arms and legs and faces. It was slightly blackened, as though by fire – except that that was impossible, because their clothes were not even singed.'

Tal had risen abruptly to his feet.

'You say their skin could not have been blackened by fire,' he said, speaking so quickly that the old man had no opportunity to reply. 'But couldn't the same effect have been caused by intense cold? I've seen young plants blackened in that way by early frosts up in the western mountains.'

Nator considered the idea briefly.

'Yes, it is a possibility. But what made you think of it?'

'I've felt that cold,' Tal explained seriously, 'down there in the Greenlands at dusk. Air so cold that Lea and I could hardly breathe.'

Now it was Nator who stood up abruptly. He went over to the open door and stared up at the stars.

'What was it we felt, grandfather?' Tal asked softly.

The old man turned around, his lined face looking more distressed than ever.

'It could have been anything,' he said evasively, 'a cold wind from the mountains, perhaps. Or even . . .'

His voice trailed away into silence.

'There was panic amongst the wild creatures,' Tal explained. 'A cold wind alone could not have caused that. No, there are things in the Greenlands that I do not understand – like the black charm which Kulok found there and now wears around his neck.'

Nator approached his grandson and placed both hands firmly on the boy's shoulders.

'That is nothing, do you hear me! A mere charm. Nothing more!'

His voice was raised unnecessarily, as though he were trying by force of words alone to dispel his own inner fears.

'That's what I thought at first,' Tal replied. 'To begin with I was worried only by Kulok's Feln-skin cloak. But today I saw the charm close up. It is not just a piece of wood or stone: it is a fearful thing.'

'No, you were dreaming!' Nator insisted, his hands shaking with agitation. 'Your imagination is playing tricks on you. Take the advice of an old man, forget these ideas. They can come to no good.'

'But they're not dreams or imaginings,' Tal replied. 'I'm sure of that. What's more, I can prove it to you. Wait here a moment.'

Before Nator could stop him, he ran out through the open

doorway and down the slope to the look-out point. His painting and the small earthenware pots in which he kept his pigments were still there, and he gathered them up and hurried back to the cave.

'Look,' he said, holding the painting out towards Nator. 'This is what I saw. I didn't know how to fill in the blank space between the foliage, and then I noticed Kulok's charm. This thing is the charm itself.'

He pointed to the squat black shape – and immediately regretted doing so. For Nator put one hand to his forehead, staggered, and almost fell. Tal quickly placed an arm around his shoulders and helped him to sit down on the low shelf cut from the solid rock of the cliff.

'Are you all right?' he asked anxiously.

'Yes, I was just dizzy for a moment,' Nator said, 'it's passed now.' But he continued to breathe far too quickly, his chest rising and falling in jerky spasms. 'Let me . . . let me see the picture again,' he murmured.

He reached out uncertainly, took the square of bark in both trembling hands, and studied it for some time in silence. When at last he glanced up, his face was deeply troubled, and there was a faraway look in his watery eyes.

'It is as I feared,' he mumbled to himself, 'the same all over again, as in the past.'

Tal placed his hands reassuringly on the old man's withered arms.

'Tell me,' he said, 'what do you fear?'

Nator stood up and shook his head, as though trying to free his mind of unwanted memories. Before answering Tal, he took a broad strip of hide from the upper shelf and wrapped it securely around the bark painting. Only then did he turn to his grandson.

'One thing at least is clear,' he said in a firmer voice. 'This picture proves beyond any doubt that you possess the Gift. But I wish to heaven you didn't, for it may well prove to be a curse, not only to yourself, but to the Clan as a whole.'

'A curse?' Tal asked, surprised. 'Why do you say that?'

But at that very moment the wooden drum sounded from the

cliff top, summoning them to Council. Without another word, Nator tucked the bark painting under his arm, doused the reed lamp, and followed Tal out of the cave. Already other aged figures were moving through the darkness, and they followed them up the stony ramp to the Council Chamber high in the cliff.

They were the last to arrive, and Tal waited while his grandfather took his place in the circle of elders. Kulok, as befitted a chieftain, was sitting slightly apart from the rest. He still wore the Feln cloak and the charm. In the flickering half-light, the charm appeared darker than ever, its blackness so intense that it seemed to dim even further the inadequate lighting within the chamber.

When everyone was settled, Tal walked to the centre of the circle and bowed to each of the elders in turn. Finally, in keeping with the ritual of the chamber, he turned to face Kulok.

'Of what am I accused?' he asked simply.

'You are accused . . .' Kulok began, and was immediately interrupted by Nator.

'Before the accusation is made,' he said quietly, 'I wish to question your right, Kulok, to sit at the head of this Council.'

Kulok turned his attention to Nator.

'Are you challenging my position as chieftain?' he asked coldly.

'No, not your position, merely your behaviour,' Nator replied calmly. 'These Councils are held whenever anyone either threatens the safety or defies the traditions of the Clan. One of our traditions is that there should be no hunting of the Feln. Moreover, there is wisdom in such a belief. The Feln, for all their mighty strength, recognize us as lords of the uplands; nor do they harm us when we venture into the Greenlands for food. Therefore what sense would there be in violating the peace which exists between us? You know all this as well as I. And yet you dare to sit in Council wearing the skin of one of the Feln. I appeal to everybody present – who should rightly be in the centre of the circle? This boy or Kulok?'

Nobody else spoke. Every eye was turned to Kulok.

'I have already told the Clan why I wear this cloak,' he said scornfully. 'But as Nator doesn't seem to have understood, I'll

24

explain it again. Six moons ago when the old chieftain, my father, died, I went alone into the Greenlands to prepare myself for the task of leadership. As Nator must realize, that is also one of our traditions. While I was there in the Greenlands, the Feln attacked me. It was they who defied our traditions, not I. And it is they who continue to violate the peace by preying on our cattle.'

'No, that's not true,' Tal protested, breaking into the argument. 'It isn't the Feln at all.'

Kulok smiled contemptuously.

'Ah, I see,' he said. 'Then would you be kind enough to tell us what did come out of the Greenlands tonight?'

Tal looked appealingly towards Nator.

'I'm not sure,' he said, 'but I think my grandfather can tell you.'

Nator didn't respond straight away. He sat very still for some time, nervously fingering the strip of hide which enclosed the bark painting.

'Well?' Kulok asked.

The old man slowly raised his head and gazed at each of the elders in turn.

'I cannot tell you anything definite,' he said. 'I can only voice my own fears.'

Again he paused, and had to be prompted.

'What are your fears?' one old woman asked.

'I fear', he said softly, his voice barely audible in the wide cavern, 'that Shadroth is risen again.'

There were murmurs of disbelief or dismay from almost everybody present. Only Kulok appeared completely unmoved by the suggestion.

'Do you expect us to take this nonsense seriously?' he said. 'What is Shadroth but a name to scare children with? Need I remind you that we are met here not to discuss foolish superstitions from the past, but to consider a serious matter.'

But if his words were intended to reassure the elders, they were noticeably unsuccessful.

The same old woman who had prompted Nator earlier now spoke again.

'You admit this is just a fear,' she said in a high quavery voice. 'What put such a thought in your mind? There has been no death cry in the Greenlands.'

'Death cry?' Kulok asked.

'It is said that Shadroth utters a death cry before he attacks,' another of the elders explained.

'Yes,' Nator agreed, 'but only when his victim is a human being.'

'And there has been no such cry,' the old woman added. 'So I repeat my question, why do you fear that Shadroth has risen?'

Reluctantly, Nator unwrapped the bark painting.

'The child who stands accused before you', he said, 'is possessed of the Gift. I have long suspected that his paintings are more than the daubings of childhood. Now I am certain of it. As you would expect of one who possesses the Gift, this picture is like an eye into the future. And here is what he sees. Judge for yourself.'

So saying, he passed the piece of bark to an elder on his right. As it moved slowly from hand to hand, there were again murmurs of fear or doubt. But no judgement was offered until it reached Kulok.

'Is this the reason for your fear?' he said, and burst out laughing. 'This smudged heap of earth in the background? Is this supposed to be the fearful Shadroth of ancient legend?'

'Do not joke when you speak of Shadroth,' Nator said sternly. 'He is no idle legend. He is nothing less than the spirit of death.'

'I'm laughing not at Shadroth,' Kulok added quickly, 'only at your pointless imaginings.'

'Then you doubt that the boy is possessed of the Gift?' Nator asked.

Kulok grew suddenly serious.

'No, I do not doubt it,' he said. 'I saw the painting this afternoon and I wondered then whether it was proof of the Gift. Ask the boy yourself.'

Nator glanced inquiringly at Tal, who nodded confirmation of Kulok's words.

'The only thing I doubt', Kulok went on, 'is your interpretation of the painting. All of you, look at it again, with fresh eyes, untroubled by Nator's fears.' He held the painting up in full view of the entire circle. 'What do you see? The legendary Shadroth? No. What the boy has painted is a conflict between a band of hunters and the Feln. And look at the Feln itself. Is that savage creature a friend to man? Could it possibly be?'

Nobody tried to answer him now, not even Nator.

'Don't you understand what has happened to this boy?' Kulok said persuasively. 'He knows the Feln are now our foes – his painting tells us that. But at dusk today, when he saw the Feln emerge from the Greenlands, his nerve failed him and he ran and hid. That is why I summoned him here tonight: to accuse him of cowardice, the most shameful crime known to the Clan.'

'No, that's a lie!' Tal almost shouted.

'Be quiet, boy!' Kulok said harshly. 'We have had our fill of empty arguments. Either give us firm evidence or hold your tongue.'

When Tal said nothing further, Kulok again addressed the elders.

'On this occasion, however, I do not propose to punish the child. He is young and must learn from his mistakes. Also, we have more serious questions to consider. Clearly the Feln are a threat and must be stopped. Therefore, what I propose is this: that a large band of hunters should enter the Greenlands tomorrow and track down the Feln which attacked the herd. Does this plan meet with your approval?'

Hesitantly, one after the other, the elders nodded in agreement. Nator was the only one who refused to be persuaded.

'Think about what you are doing,' he protested. 'To hunt the Feln will be an act of treachery. You are only agreeing to it because you lack the courage to recognize the presence of Shadroth, and because you refuse to admit what Shadroth might be. Hasn't it occurred to you that he may well be the image of your own violent desires, Kulok? Or at least a visible reflection of the cruelty and violence within all of us?'

But already the circle was breaking up, and although several of the elders paused briefly to listen to Nator's closing words, nobody supported him.

'We are agreed then,' Kulok said triumphantly.

Gathering his cloak about him, he stood up and walked over to the door. But before leaving the chamber, he paused and looked back.

'I forgot to mention', he said, 'that the boy must accompany the hunters. It will be a chance for him to prove his courage.'

4. The Bond

Nator woke Tal early the following morning. It was barely light and the Greenlands were hidden in a thick blanket of mist; but already there was movement within the cave dwellings as the hunters prepared for the trip ahead.

Still half-asleep, Tal washed his face and hands in the stone basin and afterwards crouched by the open doorway eating the gruel of soured milk and crushed fruit which Nator had prepared for him. While he was spooning the last of it into his mouth, Kulok's voice called from above:

'The hunting band will leave at sunrise.'

That was not very far off now, and Tal quickly collected the few things he would need: a roll of hide to protect him from the dew at night; a flint for making fire; a leather-thonged sling and, as ammunition for the sling, a small bag of jagged stones. He was just knotting the sling onto the belt of his tunic when Nator took something down from the upper shelf and handed it to him. This was a small round shield covered with thick leather. Snuggling inside it was Nator's own star-knife. As the name implied, this was made of five knives joined together to form a star, the long blades pointing outwards. Over one of the blades was a loose sheath which enabled the weapon to be held and thrown.

'If Kulok insists on treating you as a man,' Nator said gruffly, 'then you must go fully armed.'

It was clear from Nator's voice that he was upset about his grandson going on such a dangerous hunt. But before Tal could say anything to reassure him, a streak of yellow sunlight appeared on the distant mountains; and hurriedly kissing the old man, he went and joined the group of hunters that had already gathered outside.

A few minutes later their band was complete, and led by

Kulok they trooped silently across the hillside to where the cow had been attacked the previous evening.

The bloodstains, now dull and brown, were still clearly visible, and they had no difficulty in following them to the edge of the Greenlands; but once they penetrated the wall of thick damp vegetation, all signs of the body disappeared completely.

Impatient at the delay, Kulok signalled for three of the best hunters to comb the surrounding area in search of a trail. Within minutes they found one – in the soft earth at the edge of a clearing, the broad unmistakable prints of a fully grown Feln. They were widely spaced, showing that the animal was in full flight, and only a glance at them was enough to tell Tal what he had suspected all along.

'This animal was carrying nothing,' he said loudly. 'If it had had the weight of a cow on its back, the prints would be closer together and the paw-marks more splayed.'

A few of the more experienced hunters murmured their agreement, but Kulok turned on them angrily.

'Would you trust the opinion of a boy whose courage is in question?' he said. 'The cow was taken, and here, near by, is the fresh spoor of the Feln. What other proof do you need? Or, like the boy, would you rather turn back?'

The fear of being termed coward prevented any further protest and in silence they followed Kulok deeper into the Greenlands.

To begin with, the trail was easy to follow – the Feln in its flight had broken twigs and branches and left clear footprints in the softer patches of soil. But after the first few miles, when she had settled down to a more even pace, the signs became far harder to read. Again and again the hunters had to stop while one or two of them scouted ahead; and by the time they reached the Broad River, early that afternoon, the trail had disappeared altogether.

'This is a good place to camp,' Kulok announced. 'We will leave all but our weapons here and divide up into smaller bands to search the area. Successful or not, we will all return to this spot at nightfall.'

Tal was included in a small group that was headed by Kulok.

He guessed that the chieftain wanted to keep a watch on him, but he didn't mind now that the Feln seemed to have escaped. He even began to enjoy being in the Greenlands again – running along the narrow paths made by the antelopes or listening to the excited chattering of the tiny apes high in the tree-tops. It was a world he knew and loved, and the heat and flies which bothered many of the hunters didn't worry him in the least.

By mid afternoon they had met with no success and the men were growing tired and irritable. Kulok, who was still leading the way, gradually began to slow down until finally he stopped. Sweat was pouring from his face, and his arms hung limply at his sides.

'It is time to return,' he said reluctantly. 'Let us hope that the others enjoyed better fortune.'

Moving more slowly now, they turned towards the river – and at that moment one of the small grey alarm birds, somewhere ahead, whistled a low warning to all the creatures in the area. Tal hoped that nobody had heard it. But the oldest hunter in their group, a man named Galt, with grizzled hair and beard, immediately held up his hand for them to stop. Again the low whistle was heard, slightly over to their left.

'There is something hiding near by,' Galt whispered. 'It could be the Feln we seek.'

Without needing to be told, the hunters fanned out into the undergrowth and, bending low, crept cautiously forward. Their silent progress soon brought them to a patch of open ground and here they paused, waiting for Kulok to give the signal to advance. Tal was crouching in the lush grass, half-hidden by a thorny bush. Like everyone else, he had drawn his star-knife from the inside of his shield and was looking along the line towards Kulok. The young chieftain had taken a pace or two into the open, to where he could be clearly seen. His arm was raised and he was just about to motion everybody forward. But before he could give the signal, a series of shrill cries rang out in the vicinity of the river.

It was one of the other hunting parties and their shouts and whistles of excitement made it plain that they had raised some sort of quarry. Even more important, they were coming directly towards Kulok's band. Tal instinctively tightened his grip on his shield, feeling tense and unhappy at the way things were turning out. Kulok, he noticed, had stepped quickly back into the cover of the trees. Everyone's attention now was fixed on the thick undergrowth which ran like a solid green wall across the far side of the open ground.

They didn't have long to wait. While the other hunters were still some distance away, there was a blur of movement, like a flash of yellow sunlight in the shadows, and a great tawny shape burst out into the open. Tal recognized her immediately as the large female Feln he had confronted on the previous evening. She had no distinguishing marks, but he had looked too deeply into those clear yellow eyes to be mistaken.

She paused briefly, her shiny body unevenly banded by the long afternoon shadows that streaked the ground all around her. Then, with a low growl, she moved slowly towards the line of waiting hunters. Not until she was almost upon them did she realize the trap into which she was walking. Probably she would not have realized her error until it was too late if it hadn't been for Tal. Glancing sideways to ensure nobody was watching him, he turned his star-knife slightly so that the bright blades glinted in the sunlight.

The flash of metal caught her attention straight away; and before any of the hunters could even stand up, she had whirled around and was loping back over the way she had come. But now there was no escape in that direction either – already the fastest runners in the other hunting party had reached the edge of the open ground and were barring her way. Again she whirled around, only to find that Kulok's men had left the cover of the undergrowth and were advancing towards her. There was nowhere left for her to turn. Even as she growled and hesitated, the hunters formed a circle and, with shields held out before them, began slowly closing in.

Tal had leaped up with the rest of his group and taken his place in the circle. Although he hated what was happening, it seemed there was nothing else he could do to help the Feln now. A few more seconds and it would all be over.

While he was thinking this, half-wishing for it to be finished quickly, the man on his right hurled his star-knife at the crouching Feln. The glittering weapon travelled almost faster than the eye could follow, whirring as it spun towards its living mark. But for all its speed, the Feln was faster: in a single sinuous movement, she leaped aside, flattening herself to the ground, so that the razor-sharp blades flashed past her, only just missing one of the advancing hunters.

For the first time, the circle of hunters faltered. A few even stopped and would have backed away if it hadn't been for Kulok.

'Keep hold of your weapons and close in,' he commanded, his voice hardly more than a hoarse whisper. 'Wait until you are so near that you cannot miss. That will be the time to strike, all together.'

Again the men began their slow advance. Up until now, the Feln had remained in a crouching position, her long canines bared in a snarl of defiance. But all at once she stood up and looked round the circle, as though searching for something or someone. Her eyes flicked from face to face and came to rest at last on Tal. There followed a fleeting period of strange calm in which Tal noticed how the Feln's tail swished rapidly from side to side – once, twice, three times. From somewhere near by he heard Kulok's warning voice:

'Stand firm!'

And a moment later the Feln was charging straight towards him, her loud roar drowning out everything else as she hurled herself forward.

It all happened so quickly that Tal had no time to feel afraid. Nor did it occur to him to throw the star-knife. In the brief instant before he felt the impact of her massive body, he could think of only one thing: that this scene of which he was now a part was almost identical to his own painting, the one he had finished only the previous afternoon. Which meant that his grandfather was right: he did possess . . .

He never completed that particular thought. With a thump that jarred him from his head to his heels, the Feln charged into him, knocking the shield from his outstretched arm and sending him tumbling backwards through the thick clumps of

33

grass. When he finally came to rest, he was lying on his back, straddled by the powerful forepaws of the Feln. Yet once again he felt no real terror: he was too amazed at finding himself still alive. The Feln hadn't struck at him with her long sharp claws, which was her normal method of attack; she had merely bowled him over. And now she was standing over him, as though he were the hunted creature and she were there to protect him from his own people.

Hesitantly, he looked up at the huge jaws only inches from his face. The Feln was already watching him, and with a shock he detected in her yellow eyes the same familiar response that he had encountered before. Again there was no hint of anger or cruelty in those brilliant depths, only an unmistakable look of recognition; the way one close friend or companion might stare at another.

Almost without realizing what he was doing, Tal reached up with his free hand, more in a gesture of gratitude than anything else. But before his fingers could touch the warm muzzle, someone shouted a warning – and he became suddenly aware of figures darting desperately to and fro just at the edges of his vision.

'Don't throw it!' a voice said frantically. 'You might hit the boy!'

'But she'll kill him!' another voice answered.

'The star-knife, Tal! In your right hand. Use it! Now is your chance!'

Even in that situation Tal understood what Kulok meant by this being his chance. He flexed the fingers of his right hand and discovered to his surprise that what the young chieftain said was at least partly true – he was in fact still holding the star-knife. Slowly, he raised his arm until the sharp blades brushed lightly against the Feln's thick golden fur. But to kill her, to thrust one of those vicious points into her warm living body, was unthinkable. She had spared his life; and more than that, they had twice stared into each other's eyes. There was a kind of bond between them – a bond which was in some way connected with his own painting and with Kulok's determination to exterminate the Feln.

34

These ideas passed through his mind in a flash. The business of the painting and Kulok's strange behaviour were still a puzzle to him. Yet for all that, he understood as if by instinct where his duty truly lay. And deliberately he relaxed his grip and allowed the star-knife to fall harmlessly into the grass.

He heard a hiss of frustrated rage over to his right. There was no need to look: he knew who had made that sound. But he turned his head just the same – in time to see Kulok, down on one knee, drawing back his arm.

'No!' someone shouted. 'Be careful of the boy!'

Despite his rage, Kulok must have realized the danger too, because the star-knife, when it sped whirring from his hand, was aimed a fraction too high; and instead of lodging in the Feln's throat, it did no more than clip the top of her neck, lifting the skin before it ricochetted away into the trees.

In a futile attempt to protect the great beast, Tal had thrust his hand up onto her powerful neck. He felt the wind of the star-knife just above his fingertips and the Feln flinch as the blades struck her a glancing blow. 'You fool,' he wanted to shout at Kulok. But before he could open his mouth, his raised arm was knocked aside. He had a hazy impression of something racing rapidly over his head, and suddenly the Feln was gone, vanishing back into the heavy growth of the Greenlands as silently as she had arrived.

There was a momentary silence and several of the hunters ran forward, intending to help Tal to his feet and make sure he was unharmed. But Kulok prevented them.

'Leave the boy alone!' he ordered sharply.

Nobody thought to disobey him. Everyone knew already, without having to be told, why that order had been given: amongst the people of the Clan, there was no more unforgivable crime than cowardice.

'Take his shield and star-knife from him,' Kulok added. 'He is not fit to be a warrior of the Clan.'

Tal stood up and faced the young chieftain.

'How could I kill her?' he said quietly. 'She did me no harm.'

'No harm!' Kulok said with a contemptuous laugh. 'If I

hadn't frightened her off, you wouldn't be standing there now. She would have taken your worthless life.'

'She had chance enough to kill me,' Tal said doggedly. 'I tell you she's harmless.'

'We have heard these excuses before,' Kulok replied shortly. 'We'll have no more of them. You have again failed in your duty and your word cannot be trusted. You will take no further part in the hunt. Tomorrow morning you will return to the cave dwellings, there to await the judgement of the Clan. And this time you must expect no mercy.'

Tal turned, with a gesture of appeal, to the rest of the hunters: but their frowning faces showed all too clearly that most of them shared Kulok's disapproval.

5. Death Cry

It was late afternoon by the time they reached their camp beside the Broad River. The other hunting parties had already arrived and they gathered around Kulok, eager for news.

Tal, who was only too well aware of how Kulok would describe his part in the hunt, didn't wait to listen to the talk. While the others discussed their experiences of the afternoon, he went off alone and busied himself lighting a fire.

He felt miserable and left out; and although he was sure in his own mind that Kulok was wrong, he couldn't help smarting under the public disgrace to which the young chieftain had subjected him. His one consolation was that the Feln was still alive, roaming free somewhere out in the Greenlands. That, surely, was a kind of victory, something to be glad about, regardless of anything Kulok might say to the contrary. He tried to concentrate on that idea in order to cheer himself up. After all, it was the Feln's life which mattered most.

For a while, that made him feel happier. But a little later, when he noticed how everybody pointedly ignored him, his misery soon returned. The other hunters talked amongst themselves as though he wasn't present, refusing even to glance in his direction, all but a few of them determined to have nothing to do with a boy who had proved himself a coward and failed in his duty as a hunter. It was a humiliating experience for him, being so rejected, and rather than endure that kind of treatment, he left the camp and wandered down towards the river, searching for fallen branches and logs that he could drag back to the fire.

The camp itself was sited well back from the river, above the level of the damp mists which always rose in the early hours of the morning. Before he reached the actual river bank, therefore, Tal had left behind him the sounds of camp activity. By then it was almost dusk, the Greenlands hushed and still; and for the first time in several hours he lost some of his tension and breathed a sigh of relief. Here at last was a loneliness he could cope with, which he positively enjoyed. Nobody to accuse him here. Just himself amidst the silence of the Greenlands. Nothing else stirring, nothing . . .

Suddenly he stopped. He had been so taken up with his own problems that he had not paid proper attention to his surroundings. Now, abruptly, he put everything else out of his mind. Something was wrong, different from normal. His senses told him this long before he was able to pinpoint the cause of his unease. Yes, that was it, he had it now – the strange silence. Unnatural. There was the usual background murmur of the river, but that was all. Nothing more. Not a single bird call; not a breath of wind; not so much as the rustle of a leaf.

Tal felt a shiver of apprehension pass through him. His initial impulse was to turn and run back to the camp, but he resisted the temptation, remembering what awaited him there. No, better to endure this eery silence than to face the contempt of people he had known all his life.

That resolve taken, he unknotted the sling from his belt and continued noiselessly along the path. Within a minute or two he reached the river. The sun had long since set, but there was just enough light remaining for him to see the far shore. Between him and that shore, the dark water slid smoothly past, gently rustling the broad band of coarse reeds which lined the banks. Tal crouched down and peered across the surface of the water, watching for the tiny soft-winged flies and moths which usually hovered in the fading light, his ears straining to catch the tell-tale sound of leaping fish. But on this particular evening the deathly hush remained unbroken, the dusky atmosphere strangely empty. The river alone continued in motion, sullen and black, the invisible current tugging at the reeds. Everything else was completely still, as though waiting for the night – the sky gradually darkening overhead, while deep pools of shadow slowly gathered beneath the trees which arched out over the water.

Involuntarily, Tal found himself recalling his experience of the previous evening, when he and Lea had entered the Greenlands together. Then, the trees and bushes had been alive with sound and movement; but there had been a short period of unearthly silence just before the arrival of the icy wind or presence. Could this be the same kind of threatening calm? There was one sure way of finding out, and Tal held his breath and waited.

As the minutes passed, the shadows beneath the trees grew steadily darker, eventually enveloping the trees themselves; imperceptibly, the sky changed from grey-blue to black; the opposite shore, at first a hazy uncertain outline, disappeared altogether. Finally nothing could be seen but a faint glimmer from the surface of the river and the dark outline of tree-tops against the starlit sky. And still nothing had happened to disturb the silence – no cold wind had arrived to freeze the breath in his throat.

With a sense of partial relief, Tal relaxed and began to breathe more evenly. Obviously this was a different kind of situation altogether. This time it was the hunters, perhaps even their noisy pursuit of the Feln, which had produced the silence by frightening everything away. There was nothing here for him to be nervous about. Or so Tal tried to tell himself. But in spite of all his attempts to reassure himself he continued to feel distinctly uneasy. In his heart, he knew that the hunters alone could not produce a stillness as complete at this. There had to be some other explanation.

As if in response to his own persistent fear, his mind went back to the meeting of the Council – to the talk of Shadroth. Had it all been nothing but talk, he wondered? Was Shadroth just a word, an empty legend from the past, as Kulok claimed? Or could there possibly be something here, now, which answered to that name? Something watching and waiting, obscured by the night? At the mere thought of such a possibility, all his former nervousness returned with a rush and he peered anxiously into the surrounding shadows, trying vainly to penetrate the obscurity No, there was nothing to be seen, unless . . .

He looked more carefully at the opposite shore. Could it be that in one particular spot the darkness beneath the trees was more intense than elsewhere? He rubbed his eyes and looked again. Yes, it was possible. But then it might be no more than a thick patch of undergrowth. Again there was only one thing to do – and that was to put his suspicions to the test.

With sudden inspiration, Tal selected one of the sharp stones from the pouch at his waist and fitted it into his sling. Then, whirling the sling above his head, he took careful aim and sent the stone flying across the river towards the patch of dense shadow. There was a brief pause and he listened for the noise of tearing leaves as the stone sped through the undergrowth. But what he heard instead was a dull thud – the kind of sound a stone or star-knife made when it struck a living body. Immediately following that unexpected sound, the area of deep shadow seemed to waver and shift slightly. It soon settled into immobility once again, but not before a gust of icy air had wafted across the river and lightly brushed Tal's cheek.

Without waiting to investigate any further, his heart thumping wildly, Tal turned and ran back into the cover of the Greenlands. For a while he had no idea where he was going. Blind with panic, he crashed his way through bushes, tripping over vines, climbing hastily to his feet and running on. Not until he was gasping for breath did he slow down; and only then did he realize that nothing was following him. He was alone as before, hidden by the darkness.

He stopped to catch his breath, beginning already to feel slightly ashamed of the way he had panicked. For the time being, apparently, he was safe enough. But safe from what? From Shadroth, whoever or whatever that was? Or had there never been any real danger in the first place? Shaking his head in bewilderment, he looked up at the stars to take his bearings, and made his way back to the camp.

He found the hunters sitting around a glowing fire. Cooking slowly over the red coals was the carcass of an antelope killed by one of the hunting parties. The smell of the roasting meat reminded him of how hungry he was – he had eaten very little since leaving the cave dwellings that morning – and he sat quietly at the edge of the circle, waiting, like everybody else, for the meat to be ready.

Thankfully, nobody paid him particular attention. A few people looked disapprovingly in his direction, but nothing was said; and he began to hope that he would be left to himself until the following morning when, with any luck, he would be able to slip away unnoticed. But just before the meat was taken from the fire, Kulok turned towards him.

'We'll need water with the meat,' he said. 'Take two of the leather buckets and fetch some from the river.'

Tal stood up hesitantly. The very thought of going alone to the river revived his earlier feeling of panic and he glanced fearfully at the surrounding trees.

'What's the matter with you, boy?' Kulok asked jeeringly. 'Can't you even face the darkness on your own?'

'It's not just the darkness . . .' he said, and stopped.

How could he ever explain to Kulok the kinds of vague fear and doubt which had troubled him earlier.

'I see,' Kulok said, smiling contemptuously to himself, 'it appears you are even more lacking in spirit than I thought.' He looked quickly around the circle, his eye settling on the ageing hunter who had been the first to hear the alarm bird that afternoon. 'Galt,' he said, 'you're one of the most experienced men here. Perhaps if you accompany the boy, you might inspire him with a little courage.'

Tal, his cheeks burning with shame, didn't attempt to reply. Snatching up the two buckets, he followed Galt into the darkness. For the moment at least, his fears were forgotten – anything, it seemed, was better than standing before that circle of accusing eyes.

Galt, probably sensing his embarrassment, said nothing to him, and for several minutes they walked on in silence. But just before they reached the river, Tal stopped.

'Don't you notice anything peculiar about the Greenlands tonight?' he asked.

They stood together on the narrow track, listening, as slowly the eery silence which had disturbed Tal at dusk closed in on them. If anything, the atmosphere felt more deathly and still than it had before.

'I can't hear anything,' Galt said at last.

'But that's the point,' Tal replied. 'Have you ever known the Greenlands so silent? It's unnatural.'

Although Tal couldn't see his companion, he imagined him shrugging his shoulders.

'The Greenlands have many moods,' Galt said quietly, his voice betraying the barest tremor of uneasiness. 'We have no more cause for fear tonight than at any other time. Now get on with you. You are a member of the Clan and don't you forget it. There's no place amongst us for the faint-hearted.'

And he cuffed Tal across the side of the head with his broad calloused hand. It wasn't a heavy blow: merely a warning; the automatic response of a man who had been taught since childhood to despise any suggestion of cowardice.

Together they went on down to the river. As they reached the bank, Tal stole a fearful glance at the opposite shore; but to his relief the intense black area which he had either seen or imagined earlier was no longer apparent. Slightly reassured, he waded out through the dense growth of reeds in order to fill the two buckets. It was that simple act, as he was to discover later, which saved him.

As he bent over, forcing the rim of the first bucket beneath the surface, a terrible cry rang out. He was never able to describe it adequately. It was like a voice from the grave, a long drawn-out unearthly howl that lifted the hair on the back of his neck and made him go rigid with terror. Hardly had it died away than a blast of freezing air enveloped him, stifling the cry of fear which rose to his lips. Caught in its icy clutch, he couldn't move. He felt that some invisible presence had reached out and gripped him in its deathly fist. For a seemingly endless period it held him there, powerless, while the darkness all around him wavered and dipped as he fought for life and breath. Faint, half-suffocated, he fell to his knees and pitched forward into the water – and it was then, un-accountably, that the icy shadow lifted from him and moved away.

Choking, his teeth chattering from the cold, he clambered weakly back to his feet.

'Galt,' he called out feebly, 'Galt, are you there?'

There was no reply and he waded ashore and fell face down on the grassy bank. For a while he was too shocked and exhausted to move. When he did look up, the flickering light of torches was showing through the trees. The lights came closer and a group of hunters burst out onto the bank.

Someone touched him and said:

'The boy is also cold.'

Warm hands rolled him over, chafing the skin of his body and arms to bring back the circulation. As soon as some of his natural warmth had returned, he sat up. That was when he noticed Kulok standing in the background, holding one of the torches. The black charm, as always, was hanging at his throat; but never before had it appeared so sinister. It was more than ever like a hole in the night – a dark tunnel within which the two red dots seemed to glow.

'Did you see what attacked you?' Kulok asked.

'I heard the cry and felt some kind of presence,' Tal replied, 'but that was all. Perhaps Galt . . .' He paused, sensing that something was wrong. 'What happened to Galt?' he asked quietly.

Kulok indicated that Tal should follow him back along the path. A short distance from the river they came across Galt's dead body. His skin, like the damp moss on which he lay, was covered by a white frost which glinted and sparkled in the torchlight.

'It is as Nator predicted,' Tal murmured. 'Shadroth is risen.'

6. Judgement

Nobody slept very much that night. Throughout the remaining hours of darkness they huddled around the fire, dozing occasionally, jerking awake at the slightest noise. Tal, as alert and wakeful as any of them, noticed how the Greenlands came gradually back to life during the long dark hours. His sensitive hearing detected an almost constant furtive rustling in the tree-tops and along the paths which skirted their camp. So that when the dawn finally began to show in the sky, he was not surprised by the loud chorus of birdsong which greeted it. For the time being, the Greenlands had returned to normal.

Heartened by the clamour of life all around them, the hunters stood up and stretched, throwing off their morbid fears. In the brightening day, the events of the night appeared exaggerated and unreal, more like a bad dream than something that had actually happened. In this lighter, more optimistic mood, they prepared for the day ahead. Some threw earth on the still glowing coals of the fire, others ate a scanty breakfast, and a small group cut saplings in order to make a litter on which to carry Galt's dead body.

The body itself had been left in the long grass at the edge of the clearing. And the first sight of it immediately dashed the rising spirits of the whole band. During the night, the stark frozen limbs had thawed; and now, in the clear morning air, the skin appeared brackish and discoloured, as though it had been bruised all over.

'What has happened to him?' someone asked uncertainly.

Even Kulok was visibly moved by this unexpected transformation.

'I . . . I'm not sure,' he said hesitantly.

But Tal understood only too well. He was remembering the

conversation he had had with Nator about his own parents' death.

'It is the effect of the intense cold,' he said shortly, and turned away.

Quickly, the body was lifted onto the litter and covered with large soft leaves plucked from the vines. Everyone was eager now to leave this camp-site behind them, and before the sun had risen above the hills they were hurrying back through the Greenlands.

They reached the cave dwellings at midday. A look-out must have been posted because the rest of the Clan were already assembled on the level ground below the cliff as the hunting party emerged onto the Slopes. At the sight of the litter and the covered body, many of the older people hid their faces in sign of grief. Nator was the first to approach the litter and pull aside the leaves. When he saw Galt's discoloured limbs, he sucked in his breath sharply; and then looked first at Tal and afterwards at Kulok.

'Only Shadroth could do this to him,' he said softly.

A murmur of uneasiness passed rapidly through the crowd. Mothers drew their children close against them; the older folk shook their heads sadly.

'Do you still scoff at the ancient legends, Kulok?' Nator added. 'Or is this proof enough for you?'

Instead of answering immediately, the young chieftain walked a short distance up the ramp which led to the Council Chamber. From this vantage point, he was clearly visible to every member of the Clan.

'Nator may well be right,' he began, speaking slowly and deliberately. 'Like most of you, I know little about Shadroth. I was taught as a child merely to fear his name. But without doubt there is some evil force at large in the Greenlands. Galt's fate makes that plain enough. His was no ordinary death.'

Again there was a murmur of uneasiness amongst the crowd. One young woman with an infant in her arms called out:

'What can we do to protect ourselves?'

Other voices echoed the same concern:

45

'Yes, what's to be done?'

'Can't this thing be stopped?'

Kulok held up both hands for silence, but before he could speak, Nator broke in bitterly:

'Shadroth comes and goes at will. He first appears as a shadow, and grows slowly into a huge physical being composed of flesh and blood. But at all times he is invincible. Many years ago my own son tried to hunt him down, and died in the attempt. Even Argalna, one of the greatest hunters in the history of the Clan, was powerless against him.'

'Are you saying we must accept this outrage without protest?'

The question came from Galt's wife, a short grey-haired woman called Inra, who now pushed her way through the crowd and mounted the ramp to stand beside Kulok. Her face was already slightly swollen from crying.

'Are we just Shadroth's playthings?' she went on angrily. 'Can't we even attempt to avenge my husband's death?'

'Nobody avenged my son's death,' Nator said gently, 'and so I understand your anger. But surely there is no point in sacrificing other members of the Clan. It is bad enough that one man has died.'

'But why my husband?' Inra burst out. 'Why Galt? He wasn't an evil man. What did he ever do to bring such a terrible fate down upon his head?'

'It is unwise to search for reasons or to speak of justice where Shadroth is concerned,' Nator answered. 'He is the embodiment of death, a creature who is driven by thoughtless anger and hatred. Of all the many creatures that exist, he alone is lawless. That is perhaps why he attacks the Clan: because we do at least understand the law of the Greenlands, even though we often fail to observe it.'

Nator glanced meaningfully at Kulok as he spoke these words. But the young chieftain, who had been silent and thoughtful for some time, suddenly stepped forward and put a protective arm around Inra's shoulders.

'No,' he said firmly, 'I do not believe that what Nator says is true. We know there is nothing within the Greenlands that does not answer to some law. And Shadroth is no exception.

He has come because he has been called. Someone has summoned him here.'

'Who would do such a thing?' Nator asked.

'If your eyes weren't blinded by affection,' Kulok said, 'you would see the truth as clearly as I. Think, old man, think. Who was it who first detected Shadroth's presence?'

'Do you suspect my grandson?' Nator asked disbelievingly.

'No, not Tal!' Lea called out sharply.

And her protest was echoed by a number of those present.

Tal himself was too bewildered to say anything for the moment. Up until then, he had taken it for granted that there was no longer any question of his having acted wrongly or shamefully. Hadn't recent events proved him right? And yet here he was being accused by Kulok once again. The sheer unexpectedness of it shocked him into silence.

'Yes, I mean Tal,' Kulok went on relentlessly. 'I ask you again to think. The boy knew of Shadroth's coming, for how otherwise could he have included him in the bark painting? But in spite of that knowledge, he told nobody. Likewise, on the night that Shadroth attacked the cattle, Tal realized what was happening but gave no warning.'

'You must be mad!' Nator shouted. 'How could a boy . . .?'

'Wait,' Kulok broke in, 'hear me out. There is more to tell. Last night Tal again sensed danger. That is why Galt accompanied him to the river. But only Galt was killed. The boy was passed over. Why, do you think, did Shadroth spare him? And remember, it is not the only time he has been spared: on his own admission he was down in the Greenlands the evening that Shadroth first struck.'

Now it was Nator's turn to push his way through the crowd and mount the ramp. His fists were tightly clenched, his cheeks flushed with outrage as he faced Kulok.

'Are you suggesting that Tal deliberately summoned this thing?' he asked.

'No, not deliberately,' Kulok answered coolly. 'It is what he has done that has brought the evil amongst us.'

'What he has done!' Nator said, his voice beginning to rise once again. 'How can you say such a thing? Is it even possible for a boy to do anything terrible enough to waken Shadroth?'

'What could be more terrible than cowardice, Nator? The laws of the Clan treat it as the most serious of all crimes – and not without good reason. We are a people who live partly by hunting; and to hunt successfully we need courage. Without courage, we could not survive for long in the Greenlands. The best we could hope for would be a poor, half-starved existence on these narrow Slopes. The coward therefore threatens the safety of the whole people. Is that not so?'

'I have no quarrel with the laws of the Clan,' Nator retorted, 'only with your empty accusations.'

'Not empty, Nator. Tal failed on the hunt. Ask the others who were there. Faced with the fury of the Feln, he proved unworthy.'

For the first time, Nator's confidence wavered.

'Is this true?' he said, appealing to the crowd below.

Several of the hunters nodded and then turned aside with embarrassment.

'Then you think . . .' Nator began falteringly.

He passed one hand distractedly over his forehead and closed his eyes for a few seconds.

'What other conclusion can I come to?' Kulok asked quietly. 'The boy has the Gift. You know that. He sees into the future. And what he saw was his own cowardice during the hunt. It was his fear of the future which first led him to conjure Shadroth. You have seen his painting. You know that what I say is true.'

'But is this proof?' Nator said uncertainly.

'There is further proof if you require it,' Kulok replied. 'Consider this: that shortly after each of his acts of cowardice, Shadroth appeared amongst us. That is more than just coincidence, Nator. The boy is the unwitting cause of the evil which now afflicts us.'

Throughout this whole discussion, Tal had not moved or spoken; he had remained at the edge of the crowd, watching and listening. From the beginning he had been stunned by the unfairness of the accusations made against him. But now he was becoming seriously alarmed at the force of Kulok's arguments. There was, Tal recognized reluctantly, a crude but persuasive thread of logic running through almost everything the young chieftain said. To most of those present, his extravagant claims probably sounded convincing. Already groups within the crowd were murmuring their approval; and those who had at first protested his innocence were beginning to look doubtful.

It was this threat of impending danger which eventually broke through Tal's amazement and prompted him to act.

'You are the one who is breaking the laws of the Clan, Kulok, not I,' he called out. 'The laws tell us to leave the Feln in peace, but you insist on hunting them. How can you be sure that is not the reason for Shadroth's appearance? Isn't it just as likely? Allow the Feln to roam free once again and you may well find that the evil will leave us.'

Kulok frowned slightly and fingered the black charm at his throat.

'You have heard the boy,' he said, addressing the whole crowd, 'and you must be the judge of his words. He advises us to be cautious, not to attempt anything as dangerous as hunting the Feln. But isn't that what you would expect of one who is tainted with fear? And isn't it that same taint of fear which has brought us to where we are now – with Galt lying here amongst us, dead and unavenged?'

'Yes,' Inra shouted loudly, 'what Kulok says is true. Galt is dead, struck down cruelly. This is no time to speak of fear and caution.'

There were immediate shouts of agreement from the crowd, and a number of people turned and glared angrily at Tal.

'Fear is what Shadroth feeds upon,' Kulok said, raising his voice above the growing clamour. 'If we wish to banish him, we must prove our courage as hunters. Instead of remaining meekly here on the Slopes, as Tal suggests, we must sharpen our knives and re-enter the Greenlands. When Shadroth comes again, we will greet him not with the shrinking silence of cowardice, but with the carcasses of our prey. Above all, we will challenge him with the skins of the Feln. When enough of us wear these,' he touched his own cloak lovingly, 'Shadroth will recognize that we are truly lords of the Greenlands. And only then will he depart.'

'This is nonsense,' Tal shouted. 'Shadroth is our enemy, not the Feln, not the creatures of the Greenlands.'

But his voice was drowned out by the roar of eager approval which greeted Kulok's words. Faintly, through the uproar, he was aware that Lea and Nator were also protesting, as were several of the older people present; but they too were completely ignored. Kulok had clearly swayed the Clan to his point of view. He stood now, smiling at the crowd below him, continuing to finger the black charm which nestled in the shadow of his chin.

Disappointed, and also confused by the sudden turn of events, Tal moved away from the crowd, intending to wander down towards the Greenlands where he could find some peace in which to think. But he had not taken a dozen paces when some of the younger men and women noticed his absence.

'He is trying to escape,' someone cried out.

'Don't let him get away!'

He barely had time to turn before he was grabbed roughly by the shoulders and arms and dragged back into the crowd. One young man placed both hands threateningly around his neck and shouted:

'He has to answer for what he has done to us.'

'Yes,' someone else added, 'we demand a judgement, and we want it now.'

Within moments the cry for an immediate judgement had been taken up by a hundred or more voices. A small group of the old Council members tried to object and to point out that this was not the time-honoured way of assessing a person's guilt; but their feeble cries were drowned out by the rest of the assembly. And not until Kulok raised his hand in response to the crowd did the noise die down.

'Take your hands off the boy,' he said quietly.

'Are we just going to release him?' Inra asked, surprised.

'The people have demanded a judgement,' Kulok said gravely. 'If you are patient, I shall deliver one.'

'But that is not your right, Kulok,' an old woman cried out. 'You are usurping the role of the Council of Elders. It is for them to pass judgement, not you.'

'Normally I would agree with you,' Kulok replied, 'but this is no ordinary crime. The whole of the Clan has been endangered by this boy's actions. And at times like this, when decisions must be made quickly, it is the duty of the chieftain to take over the cares of the Council.'

A clamour of approval greeted his words; and now Kulok turned his full attention to Tal.

'You have a great deal to answer for,' he began. 'It is bad enough that you have proved yourself a coward: that alone would justify a death sentence. But worse than that, you have threatened the very existence of the Clan by summoning Shadroth amongst us. For such a crime I have no option but to sentence you to . . .'

Before he could finish, Nator strode forward and pushed him back against the cliff, showing surprising strength in spite of his age.

'No!' he shouted. 'He is only a boy! It is not just to treat him with the same harshness as you would a fully grown man.'

Again some of the older people present voiced their support of Nator. And even the hunters who had been clamouring for a swift judgement nodded in agreement, sobered by the thought of a death sentence.

Kulok, sensing the slightly changed mood of the crowd, moved cautiously back to the edge of the ramp.

'Were this boy here a mature hunter,' he said solemnly, 'I should have no hesitation in putting him to death. But what Nator says is true: the people of the Clan don't take vengeance on the very young. That is not our way.'

'It's the way you intend treating the Feln,' Tal said defiantly, 'and they're as innocent as any child.'

'Here, then, is your punishment,' Kulok continued, pointedly ignoring the interruption. 'From this moment on, you cease to be a member of the Clan. You are nothing more than a servant, fit only to do the work of the old and sick. As a servant, you are forbidden to enter either the Greenlands or the cave dwellings. You will work and sleep here, on these Slopes. Is that understood?'

Tal looked desperately up at Nator, hoping his grandfather would try to save him. But the old man merely shook his head very slightly, signifying that this was not the time to argue or protest. His whole expression seemed to be saying: wait, bide your time; you have escaped with your life – let that content you for the moment.

Tal immediately lowered his eyes and gazed forlornly at the ground beneath his feet.

'Yes,' he said in a small voice, 'I understand.'

7. The Warning

The days which followed were difficult ones for Tal. Few people spoke to him, except in an unfriendly way. Even the handful of people who sympathized with him or thought he had been judged falsely were wary of voicing their opinions, fearing that they too might be regarded with disapproval. And so, feeling isolated and alone, he was forced to act the part of the lowliest servant, working hard throughout the daylight hours without a single word of encouragement from anyone.

For the most part his tasks were dull and repetitive: he chopped and carried wood, tended fires, milked and herded the cattle – going from one job to the next without a rest. By the end of each day he was tired and dispirited; and while everyone else took refuge in the lighted caves, he lay down to sleep on the open slope, with only a strip of hide to protect him from the dew in the chill hours before dawn.

Originally, he had hoped that Nator would think of some way of reversing Kulok's judgement. But the old man quite rightly pointed out that nothing could be done until the people's anger subsided and the good sense of the Council prevailed.

'It is useless to argue with Kulok and his many followers now,' he advised. 'When Shadroth goes and the Council reclaims its rights – that will be the time to appeal against Kulok's decision and to regain your lawful place in the Clan. Meanwhile, you are at least safe here on the Slopes.'

Tal appreciated the soundness of his grandfather's advice, but still he couldn't help smarting under the treatment he received. He resented deeply the injustice of his position; and even worse, he envied the hunters their freedom to roam through the Greenlands.

Expeditions set out every day now. That was Kulok's idea. Some of them hunted smaller game – antelope, the shy burrowing porcupines, even large birds or the playful squirrel-tailed apes – while others went in search of the Feln. These groups always returned before nightfall because it was no longer safe in the Greenlands after dark. Tal would watch as they came trudging back up the hillside in the late afternoon, laden down with the game they had killed during the day. Such a large quantity of meat was not intended only for the Clan. Every evening just before the sun set, men would carry one of the heavier carcasses down to the edge of the Greenlands and lay it on a low platform. According to Kulok, this was visible proof of the courage and hunting skill of the Clan. But Tal thought of it as a kind of offering to Shadroth.

For the time being, this offering seemed to placate Shadroth. There were no further attacks on the people of the Clan, nor on their cattle. Instead, at a certain time during the long dark hours, an uncanny stillness would descend on the Greenlands. There was never any noise. Yet always, in the grey morning light, the blood-smeared platform would be bare.

Because he slept outside, it was impossible for Tal to ignore these nightly visits. Probably the first of them was the most terrifying. He suddenly awoke in the darkness, disturbed by the eery silence all around him. Even before he was fully awake, he was aware of what that silence meant, and he sat up and peered across the slope. By the light of a half-moon which now hung low in the sky, he could just make out the milky-white shapes of the cattle huddled together under the look-out rock and the shadowy outline of the Greenlands. As he watched, a patch of darkness seemed to detach itself from the even line of shadow and emerge into the open. The cattle snorted, drawing in closer to the rock; and a waft of cool air, like a distant breath from some subterranean cavern, touched Tal's bare skin. He thought: this time Shadroth has come for me – and he rose cautiously to his feet, ready to flee up towards the caves in which the people now burned their lamps all night. But there was no death cry – the eerie sound which always preceded an attack upon a human being – and the sinister black shape came

54

no closer. For several seconds it hovered over the platform –
and then it melted back into the Greenlands and was gone.

Those silent visits always followed the same pattern; and
after that first night Tal felt more secure, less personally
threatened. Nonetheless, he hated and dreaded those few
moments of deathly silence. Even in the middle of the day,
when the sun was hot across his shoulders, he would suddenly
think of them and shiver with apprehension.

By contrast, his favourite time was shortly after dusk, when
Nator and Lea crept down to talk to him. Crouched together
in the open, they would hold whispered conversations about
what was happening to the Clan.

On one particular evening, Nator arrived with the news that
there was a deepening concern amongst the elders.

'They can see that the hunters are destroying the life of the
Greenlands in order to feed Shadroth,' he explained. 'Yet in
spite of all the killing, Shadroth continues to lurk out there in
the darkness. Many of the elders are beginning to wonder
what is being achieved.'

'If they called a meeting of the Council,' Tal suggested, 'they
could challenge Kulok's plan of action.'

'Twice now they have tried to call such meetings,' Nator
replied, 'and on each occasion Kulok has stopped them. He
claims this is no time to listen to the ramblings of old men and
women, that while the crisis lasts he is the only authority here
in the Clan.'

'But can't the elders protest publicly?' Tal asked.

'That would be difficult,' Nator said. 'You see, so far the
majority of the hunters continue to support his claim to
absolute leadership. They are convinced by his argument that
the elders are too slow and hesitant to cope with the challenge
of Shadroth.'

'He thinks they don't understand the situation,' Lea explained. 'He says that his plan at least keeps the Clan safe.'

'Safe!' Tal exclaimed angrily. 'Does he call being a prisoner
safe? For that is what we are, all of us – prisoners. Our
hunters have no choice but to spend their days killing; and at
night nobody dares venture beyond the Slopes. We are no

55

longer people of the Clan: we have become the slaves of Shadroth. And what will happen if the supply of game runs out, if the animals leave the plain and go elsewhere?'

'Kulok argues that we won't have to face that situation,' Lea said. 'As soon as the hunters start to kill the Feln, he thinks Shadroth will be satisfied.'

'What do you think, grandfather?' Tal asked.

The old man mused silently in the near darkness.

'I suppose anything is possible,' he said at last, 'but I cannot believe in Kulok's solution. To kill the Feln . . . There must be another way.'

'Yes, but what?' Tal asked.

They sat thinking over this question for some time, while an almost full moon rose slowly in the sky. It cast a silvery-yellow light over the whole plain, giving to the scene below them exactly the quality of peace and calm they all yearned for.

Lea was the first to speak.

'Nator,' she said in a thoughtful voice, 'you've told us how Shadroth appeared once before, many years ago, when Tal was only a baby. What did you do then? What made him go away?'

'That was different from now,' Nator replied. 'Only a few people knew of his presence – those who penetrated deep into the Greenlands. He never disturbed the life of the people and he soon disappeared.'

'Yes,' Lea said persistently, 'but what made him go?'

'I'm not sure,' Nator admitted. 'My son, Norn, and Argalna went out against him; and after that he wasn't heard of again.'

'Isn't that the answer then?' Tal said excitedly. 'The Clan must go out against him as my father did.'

'Do you want these people here to die as your parents died?' Nator asked quietly.

'But in the end won't people die anyway?' Tal argued. 'As many of the elders realize already, we can't keep Shadroth at bay forever. In any case, you never told us that Argalna was killed. Didn't he escape?'

'That is possible,' Nator replied hesitantly. 'No trace was ever found of his body, even though people searched for some time. I've often thought that perhaps after the death of your parents he left the Greenlands and went to live elsewhere.'

The old man had barely finished speaking when Tal leaped excitedly to his feet.

'Why didn't we talk about this before?' he cried. 'Don't you see, if Argalna is still alive, he could tell us what to do! He must know more about Shadroth than anybody.'

'But how does that help us?' Nator replied soberly. 'We have no idea where he is.'

'Surely we can search for him,' Tal insisted. 'Sooner or later we're bound to find some trace of him. Nobody can just vanish.'

'It is possible that he could be found,' Nator conceded. 'But how can anybody set out on such a journey at the moment? The cliffs behind us are impassable; and no one can cross the plain and climb the western mountains in a single day. Any person foolish enough to undertake this search you speak of would have to spend at least one night down there alone, at the mercy of Shadroth.'

At the thought of such a prospect, Tal abandoned the argument. But Lea refused to give in so easily.

'It might not be as dangerous as you think,' she objected. 'Shadroth can't be everywhere at once, and we do know he visits the platform each night. Isn't there a good chance that one person could slip past him unnoticed? Especially if that person is small . . . like me.'

Nator's old face, dimly visible in the moonlight, grew unexpectedly serious.

'You must put these foolish thoughts out of your mind,' he said sternly.

'But are they such foolish thoughts?' she said. 'I wouldn't light a fire and I can move as quietly as any hunter. The chances are, Shadroth wouldn't even be aware of my presence. In any case, isn't it worth the risk? If I could only find Argalna, we might . . .'

Nator waved away her arguments with an abrupt movement of his hand.

'I'll hear no more of this talk,' he said. 'You saw what

happened to Galt. That is what awaits anybody who ventures into the Greenlands after dark. Be advised by an old man: give up thoughts of escape. For all we know, Argalna may be long since dead.'

Nothing more was said on the subject that night; but later, when he was alone, Tal went back over the conversation in his own mind. The idea of searching for Argalna still seemed attractive. Such a journey appealed to him far more than his present position, and he would gladly have set out straight away if it hadn't been for his fear of what might await him in the darkness. The mere thought of facing Shadroth made him shudder. Yet Lea hadn't appeared unduly worried by Nator's warnings. She had regarded Shadroth merely as a risk – a risk worth taking, what's more. Her whole attitude reminded him of an earlier evening, when they had both come unexpectedly upon the Feln. His immediate impulse had been to run away, while she had calmly held her ground. There was no doubt that she possessed genuine courage. But surely this was different – actually to spend the night alone in the Greenlands, knowing all the time what might happen. Would she really dare to do such a thing? Or had she been talking more bravely than she would be prepared to act?

Tal mulled over these questions as he lay down to sleep that night, but not until the next day did he receive any definite answers.

It was mid afternoon and he was carrying a load of wood up to the dwellings. The day was particularly hot and humid, and he stopped about halfway up the slope to catch his breath. While he was resting there, crouched beside the bundle of dry sticks, a picture slowly began to form itself in his mind. He had no control over the picture – he could neither change it nor make it disappear – and he guessed straight away that he was again possessed of the Gift. Under normal circumstances, he would have tried to paint what he could see. Now, in his present position, as a mere servant of the Clan, that was impossible. But perhaps for that very reason the picture was particularly vivid.

He felt as though he were looking into a portion of the

Greenlands. From the quality of the light and the length of the shadows, he could tell that it was early afternoon. On the left of the scene, a broad band of water glinted in the sunlight; and running towards that water was Lea. She didn't seem frightened or distressed. At first glance there was nothing sinister about the scene at all. But as he watched it, a gradual change occurred. Amongst the trees and cascading vines on the far side of the water, a blurred outline of shadow slowly began to appear. It was not so much a shape as the suggestion of a shape; not Shadroth himself, but rather the space he would occupy once darkness had fallen – a ghostly watchful presence, almost invisible, but ever mindful of Lea's progress through the Greenlands.

With a cry of dismay, Tal leaped to his feet. He was sure now that Lea intended to go in search of Argalna – and he had to stop her, before it was too late. Leaving the bundle of sticks where he had dropped it, he hurried up towards the cave dwelling. Lea, unfortunately, was nowhere in sight.

'Lea!' he called, fearful that she might already have set out, 'Lea!'

She emerged from one of the doorways higher up the cliff.

'What is it?' she asked, puzzled by the urgency of his cries.

But just as he was about to explain, the woman who was standing guard on the look-out rock suddenly pointed down the slope.

'Look!' she cried excitedly. 'The hunters! Look!'

People came running from the caves to see what was happening. Tal, too, had turned, distracted by the excitement all around him. What he saw made his heart sink. Kulok and a band of hunters were walking in single file up the slope. Four of them were carrying a long pole: and slung from the pole was the body of a Feln. Its coat, a brilliant yellow, seemed to catch the sunlight, and for an instant Tal thought that the creature was still alive. Then he noticed how the head hung slackly down and he realized the truth.

The hunters staggered up to the look-out rock and lowered the dead body to the ground in front of the watching crowd. Tal was the first to walk over and touch it. With both hands, he rolled the massive head aside and felt the thick fur along the back of the neck. What he dreaded above all was that this might be the female which Kulok had injured on the first hunt. To his relief, his fingers could find no trace of a cut or scar. That, at least, was some consolation.

He stood up and found that Kulok was watching him.

'I, too, searched for the scar,' Kulok said. 'As you see, this isn't the same animal that attacked you. She is still out there somewhere – though not for much longer. The hunters of the Clan will soon rid the Greenlands completely of the Feln. And then we shall be free of Shadroth.'

'Do you mean to kill all the Feln?' Tal asked in a shocked voice.

'None will remain,' Kulok said. 'There is no turning back now.'

He indicated to the hunters that they should carry the huge body closer to the cave dwellings; and the crowd, still alive with excitement, followed them.

Tal, left to himself, found it difficult to think clearly for a moment. He was horrified by what Kulok had just said. To kill any of the Feln was bad enough. But all of them! To wipe them out! Somehow the destruction had to be stopped.

As if in response to his own thoughts, he heard Lea say:

'We can't let him do it! We simply can't!'

She was standing immediately behind him, her large dark eyes filled with anger and determination.

'I agree,' Tal said, 'but how are we going to stop him?'

'There is only one way,' she replied firmly, 'and that is to search for Argalna. He might be able to help us.'

'Only if we can find him,' Tal reminded her, 'and that means spending at least one night in the Greenlands.'

'I don't care,' she said desperately, 'I've made up my mind. I shall slip away this afternoon, while everybody is still talking about the Feln.'

All at once Tal remembered why he had originally gone to look for Lea. Again he pictured to himself the scene in the Greenlands, with Lea running directly towards the waiting shadow.

'But you can't!' he burst out. 'If you go out there now . . .'
He hesitated.

'Why shouldn't I go?' Lea said defiantly. 'Why not me as
much as anyone else?'

'Because . . .'

He hesitated again, realizing that his only objection, the
vivid picture in his mind, probably wouldn't be enough to
dissuade her. Yet he was convinced that if she ran straight
towards Shadroth, she would die. He hunted frantically for
some excuse, some means of delaying her, of stopping her from
going out there.

'Well?' she asked, baffled by his silence.

Briefly, he looked across the vast green plain towards the
distant mountains, as though he were surveying the familiar
scene for the last time.

'The day is already three-quarters gone,' he said quietly. 'At
least wait until tomorrow. You could set out early, at first light.'

'What do I have to gain by waiting?' Lea asked.

'You'd stand a better chance with a whole day before you,'
Tal said persuasively. 'Promise me you won't leave until
tomorrow. That's not much to ask.'

Lea pondered the idea for a moment before finally nodding
her agreement.

'All right,' she said, 'I promise I'll wait.'

Tal didn't reply. He had got from her the promise he
wanted. There was only one thing left for him to do – he could
see that clearly now.

8. Hunted

Tal didn't stop to consider what he was about to do or to work out a clear plan. He knew that if he didn't act quickly his nerve might well fail him. He was also aware that he would not have a better opportunity than now, with everybody gathered around the dead body of the Feln.

Forcing himself not to hurry, he walked casually past the crowd towards Nator's cave dwelling; and with only a brief glance behind him to ensure he wasn't being watched, he slipped in through the open doorway. He needed only two things. The first was a weapon. His sling and pouch were hanging from a wooden peg and he snatched them down and looped them onto his belt. His second requirement was some kind of thick clothing, the warmer the better. Nator's cloak, made of two thicknesses of hide, was draped across one of the rock shelves. Hastily now, because he was frightened of being discovered in the cave, he folded the cloak into as small a bundle as possible and tied it up with a leather thong.

His next task was to get out of the cave without attracting attention. There was a heap of light kindling in the corner. Piling some of this on the cloak, he lifted the bundle and the wood up together and stepped outside. He hoped that anybody looking in his direction would assume he was only carrying a load of wood.

Again he forced himself to walk slowly past the crowd, and again his luck held. Nobody stopped or spoke to him, and with the look-out rock deserted he made his way unnoticed down towards the Greenlands. At each step he expected someone to call out and challenge him; but when he reached the midway point on the slope and still nothing had happened, his confidence began to grow. Soon he was only thirty or forty paces from the lush tangle of vines and trees and giant ferns. Once within that dense green cover and . . .

It was then that Kulok called to him. He spun around guiltily and stared back up towards the crowd, but he wasn't being challenged, as he feared. The hunters had spread the Feln out on a raised slab of rock and Kulok merely wanted him to witness the skinning.

'Come here,' he shouted, 'don't skulk there on your own. Or are you too squeamish even to watch as the Feln gives up its pelt?'

Uncertain what to do, he placed the wood and the cloak on the ground before him. But that proved to be a mistake: he had forgotten about the sling tied to his belt, and someone with sharp eyes immediately cried out:

'Look, the boy is armed!'

Kulok didn't hesitate.

'Seize him!' he commanded.

Several hunters sprang forward and charged down the slope, but Tal had already picked up the cloak and scampered away. He was confident of reaching cover well ahead of his pursuers. The only thing which could possibly stop him now was a star-knife, and it was forbidden to use such a weapon against members of the Clan. This thought had barely occurred to him when a bright circle of steel flashed past his head and sliced through the thin branches and leaves directly ahead of him. Startled, he looked back over his shoulder and saw Kulok half-crouching at the very edge of the look-out rock: he was leaning forward, one knee almost touching the ground, in exactly the stance of a man who has just thrown a star-knife.

That sight drove all thought of escape completely out of Tal's mind. For the moment he was too filled with a sense of outrage to worry about his own safety. At the bottom of the slope he stopped and faced back up towards the cliffs. The pursuing hunters had also stopped, probably as startled as he.

'Kulok, you have done a forbidden thing!' he called out angrily. 'It is unlawful to use a star-knife against a member of the Clan.'

'Have you forgotten already?' Kulok called back. 'You no

longer belong to the Clan. You are a slave of the people. There are no laws to protect you here.'

As if to reinforce his own words, Kulok ran purposefully back across the rock; but this time Tal had already guessed his intention. Pulling the sling from his belt, he loaded it with one of the stones and whirled it rapidly above his head. Because of the distance he had to cover, he put all his strength into that throw. The stone flew from the sling in a shallow arc, and as Kulok turned, star-knife in hand, it struck him full in the chest. He uttered a cry of pain and surprise, and toppled forward onto his knees.

'Stop him,' he tried to shout.

But he was too badly winded to let out more than a dry croak. In any case, Tal had already disappeared. Long before Kulok had staggered to his feet, he was running swiftly along one of the cool green tunnels within the Greenlands.

He wasn't particularly worried by the idea of pursuit: because of his size, he could travel along these narrow, low-roofed trails as swiftly as any fully grown man. Just the same, he considered it best not to take any chances, and as soon as he reached a patch of firm, dry ground, he stepped off the trail. The undergrowth here was so thick and lush that it was impossible for him to stand up, but again his size gave him the advantage. Squirming under the buttressed roots of giant trees, squeezing between the thick horny tendrils of vines, down on his hands and knees most of the time, he moved in a zigzag pattern towards the north, until he struck another path leading from the Slopes. He knew this path well and he stood up and hurried on.

Now, he was not running as quickly as he had before. To remain alert was more important than anything else. His best defence was his sharp sight and acute hearing; and these senses could not function properly if he was exhausted and gasping for breath. That alarm bird, for instance, which he could hear calling on his left: it told him clearly that the hunters had taken the path further to the south and that for the time being he was secure enough.

Smiling to himself, he settled into a steady jogging run.

Although his body was streaming with sweat, he felt reasonably comfortable in the calm green shade of the trail he was following; and now, for the first time since speaking to Lea, he took proper stock of his situation. In one sense he was oddly grateful for what had just happened back there at the cave dwellings. If he had managed simply to creep away, he would have been plagued by the temptation to go back, to give up his foolish scheme; but as things had turned out there was no going back – not if he valued his life. Behind him lay certain danger, possibly even death at the hands of Kulok. Whereas who could say what lay ahead? Perhaps nothing more terrible than a lengthy search. And at least he was free once again.

With that thought to comfort him, he quickly decided on a plan of action. The path he was on ran due west. If he followed it as far as the Broad River, he could rest there for the remainder of the night; then, at dawn, make his way to the rocky outcrop above the falls. The river was extremely wide and shallow at that point and easily forded. Also, the great rocky islands that reared up out of the stream would give him some cover if he were ambushed. Once across the river, and provided he met with no delay, he should be able to cross the remainder of the plain and penetrate deep into the mountains by the following evening.

He was so engrossed by these plans that he barely noticed the passage of time. And when he next glanced up at the tree-tops he was surprised and also slightly chilled to discover how long the shadows had grown and how worn and yellow the sunlight now appeared. Already the sun was so low in the sky that he caught only glimpses of it through the trees ahead. There couldn't be more than an hour of daylight left. And after that? What awaited him in the long lonely night?

He shrugged off his sense of foreboding and slightly quickened his pace. At regular intervals he continued to glance upwards, watching as the line of encroaching shadow climbed higher and higher up the trunks of the tallest trees – until finally only the topmost branches were still catching the sunlight. It was at that point that he first detected the distant sounds of confusion and panic.

He stopped and stood quite still, listening. There was no mistaking what he could hear. It was exactly the kind of disturbance which had attracted his attention on the evening of Shadroth's first appearance: the shrill frightened cries of animals and birds fleeing before the night. The noise came closer and closer, reaching a peak just before the shadow of the western mountains passed overhead. On every side the Greenlands sprang into life as creatures large and small ran or flew towards the safety of the receding sunlight. A bright spotted snake, blind to everything but its own terror, grazed Tal's cheek and slid across his shoulder in its haste to escape through the trees. A large pink-mouthed lizard, the spines along its back erect with fear, leaped from an overhanging branch and ran splay-legged between his feet. Moments later there was a thud of hooves and Tal had to step quickly off the trail as a group of the great horned buck swept past him.

More than anything else, he yearned to flee with them; and he might well have given way to their panic had he not realized that there was no longer any safety for him in retreat. As things stood, his only chance of survival lay in remaining calm. Holding firmly to that conviction, he waited until the noise and confusion had passed and then ran on as before. But he didn't continue in a westerly direction for very long. His ears soon told him that only a narrow band of the Greenlands had been disturbed: and so, at the first opportunity, he turned to the right and hurried along a half-overgrown trail which led to the north.

Gradually the dusk deepened around him – but not so the silence. Slowly, almost imperceptibly, it gave way to the normal sounds of the evening. The night birds began to call warily from above; bats whirred through the shadows; and the noise of insects grew steadily louder. The real turning-point came when he spied a thin brown-bodied snake dangling listlessly from a branch which overhung the trail. Brown snakes, as he well knew, were the most venomous, and he had to edge carefully around it. Even so, it was a welcome sight: it told him that Shadroth had definitely not come this way; and when a trail

66

next crossed the one he was on, he turned and continued his journey towards the west.

His main hope now was that his near encounter with Shadroth had been mere chance. If that were so, he had escaped, and he should be safe for the rest of the night provided he didn't make any undue noise or attract attention to himself. With luck, he would be securely hidden in or near the reeds which lined the Broad River long before Shadroth returned.

It was while he was contemplating his future safety that he again detected the sounds of panic and confusion – this time approaching from behind. In spite of the coolness of the evening, a clammy sweat broke out on his forehead. The last vestiges of daylight had disappeared. The moon had risen, but its light, filtered through the heavy foliage, was only sufficient for him to see the path directly ahead. He knew that he could not hope to find other trails in this darkness.

Already, birds were flying swiftly overhead, screeching out their alarm. Within minutes the Greenlands would again be teeming all around him – and after that would follow the silence which he feared so much. Unable to control his own growing panic, he began beating at the thick bushes on either side of him, searching frantically for an opening through which to escape. Somewhere near by there had to be another trail! Before it was too late, he had to find it!

He ran forward, peering desperately into every pool of shadow . . . and suddenly stopped, his eyes attracted by a flicker of movement somewhere on the trail ahead. He thought for a moment he had been tricked, and he groped for the sling in his belt. But there was no trace in the atmosphere of the icy coldness he expected, nor of the deeper-than-night darkness which had betrayed Shadroth's presence before. Again something moved up ahead – a glint of moonlit gold – and then the sinuous body of a Feln slid out of the shadows. It stole noiselessly towards him and stopped only a pace away, its great eyes searching his, its huge body completely calm and still, only the long tail swishing regularly backwards and forwards. It seemed to be waiting for something. But for what? Tal stepped forward and felt along the thick fur of the creature's neck. About halfway along, his fingers discovered the hard ridge of a partly healed wound.

As though that discovery had been a kind of signal, the Feln turned and loped noiselessly off down the trail. Tal, who needed no second bidding, followed close behind. With the Feln's eyes to guide him, he felt clear-headed once more, determined not to fall into Shadroth's grasp without a struggle.

Within a short distance the Feln turned onto a trail so little used that Tal had to run bent over in order to avoid overhanging branches. More than once he was sent sprawling by the roots and tendrils which, unseen in the darkness, snaked across his path. Each time he sprang hastily to his feet and ran on. And soon, to his relief, they left the sounds of confusion behind them.

But this period of apparent security didn't last for long. They had only just turned back in the direction of the river when Tal detected the first signs of a disturbance some way ahead. While it was still little more than a distant murmur the Feln again branched off to the right. But this time, although they quickened their pace, it took them longer to shake off the sounds of pursuit; and what was equally alarming, those sounds returned, circling around behind them, even more quickly than before.

By now Tal was hopelessly lost. He could see very little in the moon-streaked shadows and he needed all his energy simply to match the pace of the Feln. Through a growing mist of fatigue, he strove as best he could to keep up, knowing only too well what awaited him if he fell behind – that same icy touch, which had gripped his body on the night of Galt's death, reaching out for him again. The prospect of such a fate spurred him on anew. Yet despite all his efforts, it soon became impossible to escape those warning cries of fear. They were constantly there in the background, clearly audible above the rapid thumping of his heart and the rushing noise which had slowly begun to fill his ears.

In his tired bewildered state, he thought that rushing noise was in his own head. But when he stopped to rest for a few moments, it continued – a dull monotonous roar – and he realized that what he was listening to was the roar of the falls on the Broad River. At last he knew where he was; and drawing on his last reserves of strength, he ran directly towards that sound.

At some point during the last desperate stage of his flight, the Feln left him. He wasn't sure when it happened: he knew only that he was alone once more. That didn't surprise him: nor did he blame the Feln. As he well knew, every wild creature had the right to defend its own life. Such was the law of the Greenlands – a law which was made plain a few minutes later as the birds and animals, whose cries had been growing steadily louder and nearer, swept past him in the darkness.

There was no question of trying to keep up with them. He could do hardly more than stumble forward at a walking pace, and all too soon their shrill cries of panic had receded into the night. He had never felt more completely alone, the unnatural stillness broken only by the thunder of falling waters. The falls must be close now: he could feel the cool spray on his face and the noise was deafening. Although he knew it couldn't save him, he was glad it was so close, for it kept at bay the deathly silence which had become so unpleasantly familiar. He wished with all his heart that it could protect him from what must follow.

But already there was a suggestion of icy cold in the atmosphere. Now was the moment for which he had carried the heavy cloak so far. Quickly, he undid the leather binding and drew the double thickness of skin close around him. He was only just in time. From near by there came a long drawn-out screeching howl, the same unearthly death cry that he had heard once before. It was followed by an icy blast that struck him full in the face; a cold so intense that it seemed to slice through his lungs, making it almost impossible for him to breathe. But although it left him gasping and choking, it didn't freeze his body – the cloak, already stiff and rimed with frost, protected him from what had happened to Galt. Again and again those icy blasts swept out of the darkness and beat against him, sending him staggering backwards, clutching with half-frozen fingers at the now rock-hard folds of leather which alone stood between him and death. The cloak felt as though it had become a sheath of cold steel which must fracture into pieces with each successive blast, yet somehow it withstood the assault. And then, just as suddenly as they had begun, those waves of freezing air ceased.

Tal was left shivering and helpless: his eyes, nose, and mouth lined with frost: his hair, stiff and brittle, glinting in the faint moonlight. He was incapable of trying to run; he was no longer even aware of the huge volume of water crashing down immediately behind him. All he could do was stand where he was and wait.

There was a long dreadful pause, as though Shadroth too were waiting. Had Tal looked up, he would have seen the reason for the delay – a wide bank of cloud drifting slowly towards the moon. It reached the moon at last, plunging the Greenlands into almost complete darkness – and that was when Shadroth advanced. The shadows seemed to stir and move, drawing together into a great impenetrable mass; and suddenly Tal found himself staring into a vast hollow of blackness. Somewhere within those dark regions, two points of red light glowed dimly, malevolent eyes watching him. It was too late to think of escape. Terror, as much as the intense cold, held him there, transfixed. Deliberately, a portion of the shadow separated itself from the rest of the dark bulk and hovered above him threateningly. Tal half-closed his eyes, bracing himself for the blow which he knew must crush him. But just as that huge column of darkness swept down towards him, a familiar dusky-yellow shape leaped across his line of vision. Shadroth seemed to waver and blur for an instant, falling back as the death-blow descended. In that split second, Tal thought that perhaps he had been saved. It was an experience of strangely fleeting joy. Then something struck him in the middle of the forehead, jolting him backwards. It was like a bolt of pure pain which seared its way through his skull. With a cry of agony, he threw off the cloak and clawed at his face. Consumed by the pain, he didn't notice how the thunder of the falls grew louder; nor how the ground slipped away beneath his feet. Still clawing at his forehead, mindless of everything but his own torment, he fell into dark space.

PART II · THE OUTCAST

9. The Mark of Shadroth

After the intense coldness of the air, the water in the deep pool beneath the falls felt almost hot. As he sank slowly into the depths, it was as though he were being enveloped in a soft comforting blanket which warmed his frozen limbs and eased the terrible pain in his forehead. At first he made no effort to save himself: he was tempted to give himself up to this soothing world of warmth and darkness where he could sleep in peace, forever untroubled by Shadroth and the demands of the future. He actually began to drift into unconsciousness, a thin stream of bubbles escaping from a corner of his mouth. But a sudden tug of the current revived him slightly, bringing home to him the danger he was in, and he struggled feebly back to the surface.

Exhausted and shocked, he lay on his back for a while, floating, allowing the current to carry him downriver, away from the roar of falling water. His head continued to throb painfully, and compared with the lightless depths of the pool, the moonlight appeared almost dazzling. It glittered on the surface of the river, creating a broad silver path that stretched straight back to the halo of fine spray above the falls. At the very edge of that silvery path of moonlight, something large and dark was bearing slowly down upon him. He didn't notice it until the last moment and then he threw up one hand, trying to defend himself. But his fingers touched nothing more fearful than the rough bark of a fallen tree.

Almost crying with relief, he grasped one of the outjutting limbs and half-swam, half-scrambled in amongst the tangle of branches and twigs. With the last of his strength, he managed to hook both arms over the main trunk so that he was in no further danger of drowning, and after that he gave himself up to the will of the river.

Throughout the rest of the night he hovered between waking and sleeping, in a state of semi-consciousness most of the time. He was vaguely aware of the tall outline of trees slipping past on either side of him; and once when he opened his eyes, the sleek, broad head of an otter was only inches from his own. But he felt too tired and sick to be startled.

He didn't become fully conscious until soon after dawn. The rocking motion which had lulled him for so long seemed suddenly to have stopped, and when he looked up he found that the tree to which he clung was lodged in amongst the reeds close to the eastern bank. Climbing shakily to his feet, he staggered through the shallows, falling repeatedly as he tripped over the thick stems of reeds. Each of the falls jarred him badly, making the pain in his head worse than ever; and he was reduced to crawling on his hands and knees by the time he gained dry land.

Kneeling in the lush grass beneath the trees, he allowed the fierce throbbing to subside before he reached up to touch his forehead. He suspected that he had sustained a nasty wound, a broad gash perhaps. But to his surprise he felt something hard, as though a solid object, like a small stone or the broken point of a knife, were lodged there. It was cold to touch, and if he put the slightest pressure on it he sent stabbing jolts of pain into his skull. Gingerly, so as not to disturb the thing, whatever it was, he grasped it with the fingertips of his right hand, steadied himself for whatever might happen, and then pulled with all his might.

Yet even his readiness gave him no protection from what followed. He might almost have been facing Shadroth once again, because the same cold wave of agony transfixed him. If anything, the pain was more terrible than the first time. The daylight seemed to dim, the Greenlands to be swallowed up by night, and in Tal's tortured imagination Shadroth was striking at him from the darkness. Mercifully, that moment of terror was not prolonged. As it flashed across the screen of his mind, he slipped sideways and passed out.

When he came to, it was already well past noon. He opened his eyes and saw Lea sitting in the grass near by; and just beyond her, at the water's edge, the massive golden body of the Feln. To his astonishment, he no longer felt any pain. His mind was bright and alert, his sight untroubled, and in those first few seconds after waking he saw everything with extraordinary clarity: the anxious frown on Lea's face; the ridge of scar on the Feln's neck; the sharp-edged shadows of early afternoon. There was something about those shadows which worried him, but as yet he wasn't sure why that should be so.

As soon as Lea noticed he was awake, she leaned forward and brushed his cheek gently with her hand.

'How are you feeling?' she asked.

He pushed himself up into a half-sitting position. The afternoon shadows continued to worry him. There was something about them, something he couldn't quite place . . . With an impatient shrug, he dismissed the thought from his mind.

'I'm much better now,' he said, grinning at her.

'But your head!' she said anxiously.

He touched his forehead, carefully avoiding that one spot which he dared not probe, feeling for traces of dried blood. But there were none.

'Did you wash it while I was unconscious?' he asked her.

She shook her head.

'I don't think it's been bleeding,' she said. 'It's not like any wound I've ever seen before. It's more like a . . . a mark of some kind.'

'A mark?' he asked, puzzled. 'What do you mean?'

He crawled over to the edge of the bank, to where the Feln was lying stretched out. In the still, shallow water amongst the reeds, he could see his own reflection clearly. Right in the middle of his forehead the skin appeared almost charred, as though something had burned him, leaving behind a black unsightly mark.

'How did it happen?' Lea said quietly.

He turned towards her and opened his tightly clenched fist. There in his palm was the small hard object he had pulled from his forehead hours earlier. It was a fragment of something, rough on one side, sharply pointed on the other – and as densely black as the charm which Kulok wore around his neck.

'What is it?' Lea asked.

'I'm not completely sure,' Tal said thoughtfully, 'but I have a fairly good idea. You see, last night I was trapped by Shadroth, up there near the falls. I was half-frozen and couldn't run any further, and he struck at me. I'd be dead now if it wasn't for the Feln.' He stroked the fur of the huge creature which lay passively beside him, her eyes half-closed against the glare. 'She leaped between us at the very last moment. That was what saved me. Instead of being crushed, I was just knocked backwards. Shadroth could only have hit me a glancing blow.'

'And that thing?' Lea asked, pointing to the object in his hand.

Tal pondered the question for a minute or two before replying.

'I think it's the point of a claw,' he said at last. 'The claw itself must be much thicker. This narrow tip is probably all that hit me; and with the whole of Shadroth's strength behind it, it snapped off and lodged in my forehead.'

'You mean it's actually a part of Shadroth?' Lea asked fearfully.

'Yes, I think so.'

'Then throw it away,' she advised. 'It's an evil thing. No good can come of it.'

He fingered the small black point hesitantly.

'You may be right,' he said. 'On the other hand, it may mean nothing at all. It might even be useful.'

'Useful?' she asked, surprised. 'How can anything belonging to Shadroth be of any use to us?'

But Tal was hardly listening: he was thinking of the black charm worn by Kulok, of how it was somehow connected with Shadroth's appearance.

'Yes,' he said, speaking half to himself, 'it might be better to keep it, at least for a while.'

And he slipped it into the pouch where he kept the stones for his sling.

'Well, if you think it's best,' Lea said doubtfully.

Tal glanced up, noticed how anxious she seemed, and grinned at her reassuringly.

'But you haven't told me how you managed to get here so quickly,' he said. 'How on earth did you know where to find me?'

'I couldn't have found you on my own,' she admitted. 'Yesterday, after you'd gone, I was worried, and so I spent the night on the look-out rock. Not long after midnight I was woken by a strange cry, very faint and far away. I think I guessed what it was even then; and when Shadroth failed to take the offering from the platform I was certain. I knew you were the one being hunted and that you might need help.'

'Why didn't you get some of the Clan to come with you?' Tal asked.

'There was no point,' Lea explained. 'Kulok has declared that you are an outcast: and after the way he attacked you, nobody dares contradict him or question his authority in case they're treated in the same way. So I didn't even bother to ask for help – it wouldn't have done any good. As soon as dawn began to show in the sky I entered the Greenlands alone – and that was when I discovered the Feln. She was close to the Slopes, waiting for me. It was she who led me here.'

Tal again reached out and stroked the thick golden fur.

'We have a lot to thank the Feln for,' he said quietly. 'She at least has helped us a great deal.'

'I hope she goes on helping us,' Lea answered. 'We'll need some kind of protection tonight if we're going to survive.'

'Tonight?' he said. 'Surely the safest course is to return to the Slopes. What else can we do now our attempt to steal away unnoticed has failed?'

Lea shook her head.

'Kulok might kill you if you go back. And I'm not at all sure that the elders could muster enough support to stop him. He tried to sentence you to death once before, and this time he might well succeed. In any case, we'd never get there before dark. We're more than a half-day's journey away and we're already well into the afternoon.'

All at once, Tal understood his own earlier concern about the length and direction of the shadows. They had told him clearly enough what he should have grasped instantly: that time was

77

pressing. Feeling impatient at his own stupidity, he stood up and looked around – and immediately noticed something else which had previously escaped him. There was something familiar about this particular place. Yes, he had it now: this was that part of the Greenlands he had seen yesterday when the Gift had possessed him. In that vision Lea had been running towards precisely this spot; and there, across the river, amongst the tall trees that towered above the water, was the place where he had sensed Shadroth's watchful presence. He could see nothing there now except a tangle of vines and stray shafts of sunlight; but later it would be different, changed entirely.

He turned urgently towards Lea.

'Listen,' he said, 'we've got to get away from here! As far away as possible!'

'Yes,' she said, 'but where can we go? You know the Greenlands as well as anyone. Where would be the safest place?'

By way of answer, Tal crouched before the Feln and pulled gently at the loose skin around her neck, trying to coax her to her feet. But instead of responding to his sense of urgency, she rolled over on her back and dabbed playfully at him with her great paws. Her deep yellow eyes appeared completely calm and untroubled.

'Why won't she help us?' Lea asked in a puzzled voice.

Tal straightened up and stepped back.

'She knows there is nowhere for us to hide,' he said resignedly. 'Last night she did everything in her power to help me escape, and still Shadroth found us. No one can hide from him, not in the Greenlands. I think she understands that now.'

'Are you saying we have no choice but to wait here until Shadroth comes for us?' Lea asked.

'What else can we do?' Tal said helplessly. 'There simply isn't . . .'

He stopped, surprised by the way the Feln leaped lightly to her feet. As he watched her, she stepped deliberately into the river and waded out through the reeds until the water reached halfway up her flanks. Then she turned her head slowly and stared at him over her shoulder.

'What is she doing?' Lea asked.

'I think she's warning us about something,' Tal said.

As though in response to his words, the Feln crouched lower in the water until only the top of her head was visible. And all at once the truth dawned on Tal.

'Don't you see what she's telling us?' he burst out. 'I should have realized it myself. On the two occasions when I've survived Shadroth's attacks, I've done so by falling into the river. The river is the only safe place!'

'You mean all we've got to do is hide out there in the deep water?'

'Yes,' Tal said excitedly. 'It protected me before. Why shouldn't it work again?'

He was so relieved and elated by his discovery that he hardly noticed how Lea failed to share his enthusiasm. Her face as serious as ever, she was looking past him, in the direction of the mountains.

'But what about our search for Argalna?' she objected. 'We can't get from here to the other side of the mountains in a single day. Sooner or later we'll have to spend a night away from the river. So why not start now? Or have you given up the idea of the search?'

Tal's initial excitement disappeared almost completely. As on other occasions, he felt slightly shamed by Lea's courage and steadiness of purpose. She was quite right, of course: their immediate safety wasn't the only consideration. They had to find Argalna and somehow rid the Greenlands of Shadroth altogether.

'Perhaps if we just took refuge in the river this one night,' he said hesitantly.

He knew how that must sound: as nothing more than an excuse, a means of putting off the evil hour. On the other hand, the mere idea of again being at the mercy of Shadroth filled him with dread.

'Listen, Tal,' Lea said gently, 'I'm frightened too, and I've never been attacked or directly threatened by Shadroth – not in the way you have. But we must be honest with ourselves: we can't achieve anything by staying here. Somehow we have to find a way of escaping. Perhaps if we travelled separately one of us might survive. What do you think?'

But Tal wasn't interested in that possibility. Something else Lea had said had already set him off on a new train of thought. 'A way of escaping,' he muttered to himself. And he pictured once more his own fall into the river and the tree to which he had clung, sick and exhausted.

'Yes, that's the answer,' he said, his excitement beginning to return. 'Why try to cross the mountains at all? Why not use the river?' He pointed to the tree which had saved him the night before – it was still there, aground in the shallows, caught up among the coarse stems of reed. 'We could float down the river on that,' he explained.

'How do we know it would take us out of the Greenlands?' Lea said doubtfully. 'Nobody has ever discovered where the Broad River leads.'

'At least it will take us far away from Shadroth,' Tal argued. 'Once we've reached a place of safety, we'll be free to go where we please. Also, isn't it possible that this is the way Argalna escaped? Remember that he had to worry about Shadroth as well.'

For the first time in some minutes the slight frown left Lea's face.

'It's worth a try,' she said.

Together they waded out through the shallows and tried to push the tree into deeper water. But it was firmly wedged on the sandy bed.

'We'll never budge it like this,' Tal said, wiping the sweat from his face. 'We need some kind of lever.'

'I have a knife,' Lea said, drawing a long blade from the sheath which hung at her waist. 'We could cut two poles and use those.'

'Yes,' Tal agreed, 'but we'll have to hurry, because it's getting late.'

The shadows were in fact lengthening rapidly. And by the time they had cut two sturdy poles and trimmed off their side branches and leaves the sun had already dropped behind the trees on the opposite bank. Tal, mindful of what awaited them in the approaching darkness, was careful not to look around, devoting all his energy to prising the tree loose of the sand and reeds. It was so firmly wedged that the two of them, levering upwards with the poles, could move it only an inch or two at a time. But very gradually it was eased clear of the shallows until at last it floated free.

Standing chest deep in the water, his heels braced in the sand, Tal held the tree while Lea scrambled through the branches and twigs and climbed up onto the main trunk.

'What about the Feln?' she asked, as she drove one of the poles into the sandy bottom in order to hold the tree out of the current.

Tal looked over his shoulder. Only a few moments earlier he had noticed the Feln standing there on the bank, watching them with her calm golden eyes. Now she had disappeared into the darkening Greenlands.

'She probably realizes we don't need her help any longer,' he said.

He wasn't sure whether he believed that himself. Even as he clambered up onto the tree beside Lea, he wondered if there wasn't perhaps another reason for the Feln's sudden disappearance. Yet whatever the reason, it was too late for them to turn back now. The evening was waning rapidly, and already the edge of the strong central current was spinning them around. Tal bore down on the long pole to prevent their being swept back into the shallows. Turning slowly with the movement of the current, he stole a furtive glance at the matted undergrowth on the far bank – at the exact spot which he had glimpsed in his earlier vision of this place. It was hard for him to be certain of anything in the vague half-light, but the streaks of deep shadow between the trees appeared far too black for that time of the evening, as though the darkness were gathering in that one spot more quickly than elsewhere. He looked away, continuing to push vigorously on the pole as the current swung them round to face downstream.

'We'll soon be on our way,' he said aloud.

But in spite of his apparent cheerfulness, he could not escape the suspicion that he and Lea were no longer alone.

10. River Journey

The night fell swiftly. On either side of them, as they were whirled along, the trees made a solid dark line against the starlit sky; but always, on the western bank, there was an area of unnatural blackness, like a deep hollow in the night. It remained directly opposite them, matching their pace, dogging their steady passage down the river. Even the rising moon made no difference to it: everything else was touched with silver-yellow light, but not that one dark space. Impenetrable, completely silent, it brooded watchfully over their journey.

Tal hoped that Lea hadn't noticed it; but before they had gone very far, she turned to him and whispered:

'It's Shadroth, isn't it? Over there' – pointing with the end of the pole.

He nodded. It was useless denying what they both knew to be true.

'I don't think he can reach us out here, though,' he whispered back. 'We're probably safe as long as we don't go close to the shore.'

The truth of that statement was made plain only a short time afterwards. They had reached a point where the river bent gently towards the south. As they followed this long curve, they were pushed steadily out of the main stream of the current and closer to the western shore. They didn't notice what was happening until the tree on which they were sitting began to spin slowly, caught up in one of the eddies at the edge of the current.

'Quick!' Lea yelled – and she leaped to her feet and thrust one of the poles down into the swirling water.

That was very nearly her first and last attempt to save them, because the water was still far too deep for poling; and instead of making contact with the sandy bottom, she found herself thrusting down into empty space. If it hadn't been for the surrounding twigs and branches, she would almost certainly have disappeared, but these supported her long enough for Tal to grab hold of her and pull her back onto the trunk.

After that, all they could do was test the depth from time to time as they were carried ever nearer to the bank; and they were uncomfortably close before their poles finally touched the bottom. There was no need for either of them to give any signal. They immediately thrust downwards as hard as they could, trying to drive the tree back into the safety of the current. It responded slowly, its great weight and bulk resisting their efforts for some time; and before it eventually changed direction and veered back into the stream, there was a gust of all-too-familiar cold air from the shore.

That was a kind of warning to them, and for the rest of the night they remained ever vigilant, standing ready with the poles if the tree showed the slightest tendency to drift in towards the shallows. Time and again they had to push for their lives, sweating and groaning with the effort, the air striking harsh and cold on the wet skin of their arms and legs. There were places, too, where the river narrowed to such an extent that even being in the middle of the current was no guarantee of safety. Shadroth's invisible presence seemed to reach out from the bank and they had to sit huddled together while the temperature plummeted around them. Fortunately, these episodes never lasted very long: whenever the river narrowed, it also ran extra fast, soon carrying them to safety.

The first time they emerged from one of these narrow gorges, Lea leaped to her feet and rubbed her skin vigorously to bring back the warmth.

'Aren't you cold?' she asked Tal.

He remained seated, a puzzled expression on his face.

'Not really,' he said.

'You must be tougher than I am then,' she replied, still shivering.

'I don't think it's a matter of toughness,' he said slowly. 'It may have something to do with what happened back there at the falls. I feel the cold, but it just doesn't seem to worry me any longer.'

'You mean Shadroth has no effect on you?'

Tal touched the wound on his forehead. In the moonlight, it showed as an intense black spot, almost as dark as Shadroth himself.

'No,' he said. 'When he's close, my head hurts, but that's all.'

From then on he always knew when they were approaching one of the narrow places: his head would begin to throb and a dull pain would slightly blur his vision until the river again opened up before them.

'You're the lucky one,' Lea said as she sat shivering beside him.

But Tal could tell she didn't really envy him. There was something both strange and frightening about his sudden ability to withstand Shadroth's presence. Neither of them understood what it meant; nor were they particularly eager to find out. They both had more than enough to concern them already. The twists and turns of the river, the uncertain course of the current, kept them forever on the alert; they knew that at any moment they might be called upon to strain at the poles, to fight the tree away from the waiting darkness.

The tension of those long hours told on them steadily, and by morning they were both exhausted. The moment the sky began to turn from black to grey, they worked the tree in towards the eastern bank, ran it firmly aground on a sandy bar, and waded ashore through the shallows. Both of them were very hungry – Tal especially, who hadn't eaten at all on the previous day. And tired as they were, they wandered along the water's edge gathering fruit and nuts which grew from the vines that twined up through the trees. The sun was well above the horizon by the time they had eaten their fill, and they lay down in the now warm grass and fell into a deep sleep.

Tal awoke late in the morning. He sat up, blinking the sleep from his eyes, and saw the Feln lying peacefully in the near-by shade.

'Here's one creature who isn't frightened of Shadroth,' he

said, shaking Lea awake. 'She must have followed us through-out the night.'

He went over and crouched in front of the Feln, who half-closed her golden eyes and yawned lazily, revealing long canine teeth and a bright red tongue. He reached out to touch her, and she nuzzled gently at his arm and chest, in a kind of greeting.

Lea had also sat up.

'It's good to know Shadroth wasn't the only creature interested in us,' she said. 'The Feln must have been watching over us just as carefully.'

That idea alone made them feel more cheerful, and they quickly bathed in the river and set about gathering food for the journey ahead.

By early afternoon they had refloated the tree and were again drifting downstream. In the hot sunlight they made no great effort to stay in the centre of the river. Most of the time they lay back on the trunk and dozed – standing up and using the poles only if the tree swung in close to the shore. During those hot bright hours, it was hard for them to imagine that the Greenlands could be anything but peaceful and friendly. Birds and small game called from the cover of the trees; and the Feln was always there, clearly in view, her coat glinting like gold as she loped easily along the shoreline.

But with the coming of evening, the whole atmosphere changed. Long fingers of shadow moved furtively across the river, and no sooner had they touched the opposite shore than the Feln disappeared, sliding back into the thick undergrowth which was her natural element. Once again, as the night took hold, the dense black shade appeared beneath the trees, waiting for them to grow tired and make an error.

As on the previous night, they had to be ever on the alert, ready at any moment to combat the shifting, treacherous nature of the current. It would sometimes hold steady for an hour or more: and then suddenly grow erratic, swinging them from one side of the river to the other, so that for the next hour or two they spent all of their time frantically poling themselves free of the shallows.

Those periods of anxious activity had different effects on both of them. Lea emerged from them shivering with cold, but otherwise reasonably calm and steady. Tal, unaffected by the cold, always felt shaken and sick, and he would crouch down on the trunk, holding his head in both hands, waiting for the fierce throbbing pains to subside. Not surprisingly, neither of them was disposed to waste precious energy on unnecessary discussion. Only once, in fact, did they think or talk about anything other than the immediate problem of trying to stay alive. It was during a quiet period when they were sitting close together near the end of the log.

'One thing keeps puzzling me,' Lea said abruptly.

'What's that?'

'I can't help wondering why Shadroth is following us all this way. Why us? Why doesn't he go back to the Slopes? He'd find plenty of people there.'

'But we're the only ones who are unprotected,' Tal said. 'If he went back to the Slopes, everybody would be safe inside the cave dwellings.'

'Yes,' Lea admitted, 'but that hasn't always been true. I spent a night on the look-out rock, remember; and you slept outside every night after your return from the hunt. He had plenty of opportunity to come for us then. But he didn't. So why is he so interested in us now?'

Tal felt too harassed and tired to consider such complex questions.

'You might say the same about the Feln,' he replied irritably. 'Why is she following our every move?'

'But isn't that really the same point?' Lea said. 'What makes us so important all of a sudden? To either Shadroth or the Feln?'

'Perhaps it was what happened to me at the falls,' Tal suggested vaguely. 'I can't think of anything else.'

'You may be right,' Lea said hesitantly, 'in fact I'm sure it's partly the reason. But I don't think it's the whole truth. After all, the Feln came to your rescue before you received that wound.'

She glanced quickly, uneasily, at the sinister black mark on Tal's forehead.

'Then why do you think they're following us?' Tal asked.

'I'm not sure,' she said slowly. 'It could be something to do with the journey itself. Maybe it's important in some way we don't ...'

Before she could finish, the tree suddenly dipped and swung beneath them, spinning rapidly out of the central channel; and from then until dawn they had neither the time nor the opportunity to continue their conversation.

When, in the grey light of day, they again grounded the tree and walked ashore, they were as tired as they'd been on the previous morning. But after a good sleep, and waking to find the Feln watching over them as before, their spirits rose. Their plan, it seemed, was working. They had survived two nights – why not more? Sooner or later, Shadroth would have to give up and admit defeat. They felt sure of that. And when they took to the river for the third time, they did so with a renewed sense of confidence. It was their confidence, perhaps, which led them to disaster.

They noticed in the course of the afternoon that the mountains on either side had become lower and nearer – very different from the bare towering peaks which closed in that part of the plain where they had spent all their lives. What they could see now were little more than hills which seemed to curve around and meet at a particularly low point some way ahead of them. It was towards that dip in the hills that the river was flowing. Instead of turning and twisting as it had done, it ran straight and true. And throughout most of the night they had almost nothing to do except sit and watch as the strong central current carried them ever closer to the edge of the plain.

As hour followed hour, they grew tired of watching for shifting patterns in the current. For a while they talked in whispers. Then, later, they sat back to back, checking only occasionally to make sure they were on course. By then the hills were very close, and Tal wondered what they would find there – another waterfall? – rapids perhaps? They would know soon enough. He felt Lea slump slowly against him and guessed she had dozed off. He thought: let her sleep; she might need all her energy for what lies ahead. As long as he remained awake nothing could go badly wrong. The important thing was for him to stay on the alert.

He had that idea clearly in his mind when he closed his eyes. His intention was to relax only for a moment; but somehow he, too, dozed off, slipping easily into a dream which closely resembled his waking state. In the dream, he was standing at the front of the log watching over the sleeping Lea. She was groaning softly and he couldn't understand why. He kept telling himself: there's nothing to worry about, she's safe while I'm here, quite safe.

He was still mumbling those words when he suddenly started awake. He had no way of knowing how long he had been asleep. Beside him, Lea was making a peculiar moaning noise; and his own head was throbbing painfully. He leaped up, expecting to see the broad stretch of the river. But the river was gone. The trees on the western shore towered above him, and there, close at hand, in the deepest shadow, he could see a blur of darkness out of which two blood-red eyes gleamed maliciously. In that split second of confrontation, he was aware of only one thing: not of the cold or the overwhelming danger. What he sensed was far more basic than that: it was a blast of sheer hatred which swept over him like some invisible force whose only purpose was to destroy him utterly. He would not have thought that such a loathing was possible if he hadn't experienced it. At that moment he knew with absolute certainty that Lea was not Shadroth's immediate object. He, Tal, was Shadroth's true target and enemy, the one person above all others whom the dark creature sought to crush.

Behind him, Lea, unable to breathe properly in the bitter cold, began to gasp and choke. That sound broke the spell which gripped Tal and he groped blindly in the darkness. The smooth bark of the pole, when he found it, was already covered with frost, warning him that he had very little time. Ramming it down onto the sandy floor of the river, he pushed with all his might. For one long moment he felt as though he were resisting the full weight of the tree. His legs began to tremble, his arms and back to bend and give under the strain. Then, very slowly, the tree turned and changed direction. He pulled the pole closer and pushed again. Already the throbbing in his head was growing weaker. And at the third heave on the pole, an eddy caught the tree and carried it safely back towards the main current.

He knew there was not a second to lose. Dropping the pole, he crouched beside Lea. Her hair and skin were thinly coated with white frost, but now that they were back in the warm night air she was breathing freely again. Pulling off the light tunic which covered the upper part of his body, he wrapped it around her and immediately began to chafe the bare skin of her arms and legs. Gradually the stiffness went out of her muscles and a little of the natural warmth returned. Relieved, he leaned back on his heels, his own hands and arms aching with the effort he had just made.

Only then did he fully recognize the nature of the noise which had been growing in the background. He peered ahead. The hills were almost upon them, sloping steeply down to form a ragged, narrow gap. The noise that he could hear was not the dull crashing of a waterfall, but rather the continuous rush of rapids. That, at least, was something to be thankful for; and he picked up the pole and stationed himself at the end of the trunk, ready to guide the tree as best he could through the broken water ahead.

But just before they were swept into the gorge, he noticed something else which drove all other thoughts out of his mind. Up there, spanning the rock on either side of the defile, was the now familiar black image of Shadroth. Outlined against a sprinkling of stars in the night sky, he appeared huge and strangely formless. As his terrible death cry rang out, Tal abandoned his position at the end of the tree and ran forward to throw himself over the still unconscious body of Lea. It was the only protection he could offer her and he had no idea whether it would be sufficient.

Seconds later the tree, caught up in the rapids, was bucking and spinning its way through the freezing air. Tal, surrounded by noise and darkness, dug his fingers and toes into the rough bark of the trunk, determined not to be thrown off. Beneath him, the passive body of Lea lay quite still, while on every side water and rocks smashed together in blind chaos. Flecks of foam, torn from the tops of waves, froze in mid air, falling onto his back as chips of ice. Again and again he was jolted violently as the tree, plunging and rearing, crashed against the side walls of the gorge, bouncing off and sliding dizzily back into the churning waters. Soon, Tal had lost all sense of time and space. Sideways or forwards, up or down, before or after – such things meant nothing to him any longer. He kept only a single idea clear in his mind: that at all costs he must hold on. Clenching his eyes tight-closed against the throbbing pain which signalled Shadroth's nearness, he concentrated all his strength into his hands and feet, and simply waited – waited for the darkness to lift and for the noise and confusion to disappear.

The silence and calm, when it arrived, did so quite abruptly. The rush and movement were suddenly left behind and the tree was again out in the open river, gliding smoothly across unbroken water.

Tal rose stiffly to his knees and shook the ice from his hair. Lea still hadn't moved. Those signs of warmth which he had detected in her limbs earlier were now gone. She lay before him cold and stiff, her face and body frozen into stillness.

For the first time since setting out on the river journey, Tal gave way to panic.

'Lea!' he called wildly, 'Lea!'

Desperately, he took her by the shoulders and shook her, trying to force her back to consciousness. But she made no response. Her eyes remained closed and there was no trace of breath from her mouth or nostrils. Tearing aside the tunic which he had wrapped around her, he put his ear over her heart and listened. For what seemed a long time there was nothing. Then, when he had all but given up hope, he heard the faintest possible murmur. It was like a distant fluttering, uneven and erratic, so light that it was almost drowned out by the anxious beating of his own heart. She was just barely alive – but for how long, he couldn't tell.

11. The Gentle Folk

For the short remainder of that night, Tal lay close against Lea, trying to revive her with the warmth of his own body. Shadroth had not appeared again since they had emerged from the gorge. It seemed that the ring of mountains surrounding the Greenlands formed a natural barrier beyond which he could not venture. Yet that was now small consolation to Tal, who would rather have had Lea alive than this safety which had come too late.

When day broke, she was still unconscious, the skin around her lips and nostrils pinched and blue with cold. Sliding carefully out from under the tunic which covered them, Tal stood up to survey this unknown country to which they had come. To his astonishment, it was nothing like the Greenlands. Gone was the thick forest of trees and coiling vines which he had been used to: in its place there was now an endless vista of rolling grassland.

Some way ahead, near a bend in the river, he could see what appeared to be a cluster of clay or earth mounds. As they came closer, he realized they were dwellings of some sort because there were people moving in amongst them. It was what he had been hoping for ever since they had emerged from the gorge, and grabbing one of the poles he thrust it down into the water, feeling for the bottom. At that point the river was still too deep, but as they approached the bend, the tree was swung out of the main current and he was able to pole it ashore only a short distance downstream from the village.

Leaping into the shallows, he took Lea in his arms and carried her up the bank and into the waist-high grass. Already a group of villagers was coming down to meet them. They were small people with dark brown skins and large curious eyes. Unlike the people of the Clan, they carried no weapons, but Tal hardly noticed this as he staggered towards them.

'Quick!' he said. 'She needs warmth and shelter.'

Gentle hands took Lea from him and carried her off to the village. He followed anxiously behind, watching to see that no harm came to her. But it was soon obvious that he had no cause for fear. People ran from the huts with clay baskets filled with live coals and built a small circle of fires. Others brought rugs made from a soft warm material which Tal had never seen before. Lea, still cold and unmoving, was wrapped loosely in these rugs and placed carefully within the circle of fires. Meanwhile, other fires were built near by and over these were suspended large cauldrons of water.

So far nobody had paid any attention to Tal, but now an old woman, whom Tal had heard the other villagers address as Molani, turned towards him. Her hair was completely white and she was so bowed over with age that she had to support herself with a stick.

'The rugs and fires alone will not save her,' she explained. 'When the water is heated, we will place her in it. Then we shall see.'

Her voice was quiet and controlled, yet not unkind.

Tal nodded and stood there waiting, never once taking his eyes from Lea's face. The minutes passed with painful slowness and, as Molani had predicted, she showed no signs of revival. But by now the water was simmering over the fires. Several of the cauldrons were quickly emptied into a shallow tub and Lea was gently lowered into the warm water. Tal moved forward and crouched beside her, watching for the slightest movement. But she continued to lie as still and silent as ever.

'It's all useless!' he burst out bitterly, giving way to his deepest fears. 'See for yourself, it isn't working! Nothing can bring her back now!'

He put his hands over his face, fighting back the tears which sprang to his eyes. But Molani touched him lightly and encouragingly on the shoulder.

'Be patient,' she said, 'it will take time. Observe carefully and you will see the change.'

Again Tal waited, though without any great hope. While others added more warm water to the tub, he stood miserably to one side. He couldn't help recalling the way Galt had looked when they had found him: he too had lain straight and still, exactly like Lea now; and he had never recovered.

Yet in spite of Tal's feeling of hopelessness, a slow change was occurring in Lea's appearance. Very gradually the skin around her mouth lost its pinched bluish appearance; and a pink flush of life and warmth began to spread over her cheeks. From then on, her recovery was rapid; and, to Tal's delight, within minutes she was breathing evenly and deeply once again.

'She's going to be all right!' he said happily.

He leaned over as if to wake her, but Molani restrained him.

'She is in a deep sleep now,' she said, 'and we mustn't disturb her. She has been close to death and must rest if she is to recover fully.'

Tal drew back as Lea was lifted from the tub and put onto a litter. Warm rugs were spread over her and she was taken to the nearest of the mud dwellings.

'Will it take long for her to recover?' he asked.

The old woman hesitated slightly before she answered.

'Have no fears for her safety,' she said at last. 'You may continue your journey knowing that she will be well cared for.'

'But I'm not going on without her,' Tal objected. 'I'll stay here until she's strong enough to come with me.'

Immediately there was a murmur of uneasiness amongst the assembled people. Someone in the crowd said quietly:

'It would be dangerous for us to harbour him.'

Puzzled by this unexpected response, Tal looked at the circle of faces. He saw no hatred in their eyes – merely a suggestion of fear.

'I don't understand,' he said. 'Why should you think me dangerous? I have done you no harm.'

'Aren't you one of the Clan people?' Molani asked.

Tal nodded.

'Then that is why we fear you,' she said.

'But why me?' Tal protested. 'What have I done?'

'It is not what you may have done which worries us,' Molani explained: 'rather it is what you represent. You see, we are known throughout this region as the Gentle Folk. We do not hunt, neither do we carry weapons. You, however, are of the Clan. And in the minds of my people the Clan is always associated with violence. We are frightened you will bring this violence upon us.'

Tal gazed helplessly across the rolling Grasslands. After the terrors of the night and his anxiety over Lea, he felt exhausted, unable to cope with this new challenge.

'How can I harm you?' he said wearily. 'I am one against many. And you have just shown me great kindness' – he gestured towards the hut in which Lea now lay sleeping. 'What possible violence could I bring upon you?'

'Any form of violence disturbs us,' Molani said. 'But in particular we fear Shadroth. He has never yet ventured into the Grasslands; and if it is in our power to do so, we shall prevent his ever crossing the mountain barrier.'

'And you think I might lure him here?' Tal asked.

'Yes, you or the girl. That is why she too must leave once her strength has returned. You are both members of the Clan. And what is Shadroth but a reflection of the violence which dwells in the heart of all your people?'

'But Shadroth is my enemy!' Tal burst out. 'We have fled from him!'

'Then why do you bear his mark upon your forehead?' Molani asked sternly. 'Such blackness, deeper than the night itself, can be implanted only by him. And the girl as well: she arrived here cold and silent. She, too, had been touched by Shadroth.'

'No, you don't understand,' Tal began, 'we don't serve Shadroth, we want to destroy him. We are searching for a man called Argalna, because . . .'

He stopped, unsure of how to go on. How could he possibly explain, when there was so much he didn't understand fully

94

himself? More than anything else, he wanted to lie down and sleep, and momentarily he closed his eyes which felt sore and gritty from fatigue. When he opened them, a man had stepped out of the crowd and was standing beside the bent figure of Molani. He was middle-aged, with greying hair and beard. He was slightly taller than most of those present, and his skin, although deeply tanned from exposure to the sun, was perhaps lighter in colour – but otherwise he appeared no different from the rest of the Gentle Folk.

'You wish to question the boy, Ubek?' Molani asked, addressing him.

He nodded and directed his gaze at Tal.

'You claim you are searching for Argalna,' he said. 'Is this true?'

'Yes.'

'Throughout the Grasslands,' Ubek said, 'he is known as a man of peace. What do you want with him?'

'I have heard that he is also a mighty hunter,' Tal replied. 'It is said that many years ago he defeated Shadroth. That is why I wish to find him, to get help and advice.'

'Have you been sent on this journey by the elders of the Clan?' Ubek asked.

'No, I do not dwell on the Slopes any longer,' Tal answered. Even here, miles from his home, it hurt him to make such an admission, but he forced himself to continue: 'I am an outcast of the Clan, rejected by them. That is partly why I bear Shadroth's mark on my forehead. He caught me in the Greenlands at night and nearly killed me. I survived only by falling into the river.'

Ubek pulled thoughtfully at his lower lip.

'Then you have no friends in the Greenlands?' he asked.

'Only a few,' Tal explained. 'My grandfather and some of the elders believe I've been treated unjustly – but hardly anyone else. Though in the Greenlands itself there are the Feln who ...'

'The Feln?' Ubek broke in. 'They are your friends?'

'Without the Feln's help, we could never have escaped,' Tal said.

He was about to go on and explain what had happened, but Ubek had already turned towards Molani and the rest of the crowd.

'In my opinion,' he said quietly, 'the boy is not a danger to us. It might prove much more dangerous, both to us and to him, if we cast him out.'

Uneasy murmuring again broke out amongst the people.

'I understand your fears,' Ubek went on, 'but there are times when fear alone cannot defend us.'

'What then would you advise us to do?' Molani said.

Ubek considered the question for several moments.

'One thing should be clear to everyone,' he said, weighing his words carefully. 'Shadroth is risen again. The boy's wound, the girl's condition, leave no room for doubt. As everyone knows, Shadroth is never defeated without a struggle. My advice, therefore, is this: let the boy remain here a while longer. He, too, needs rest. After he has slept we can test the truth of his words and decide how best to act. Remember that Argalna himself once sought sanctuary here. It may well be that this boy has as much right to make a claim upon us.'

There was a short silence before Molani nodded her approval.

'It is agreed,' she said. 'We leave the matter in your hands, Ubek.'

As the crowd dispersed, Ubek gathered up one of the soft rugs which he took down to the river bank and spread out on the dry sand.

'The skin on your back is scarred from Shadroth's cold,' he said quietly. 'If you sleep here in the open, the sun will heal you.'

He was about to leave, but Tal reached out and detained him. Despite his fatigue, Tal was thrilled by the idea that Argalna had stayed at this very village.

'Do you know where Argalna went when he left here?' he asked.

Ubek waved the question away.

'We will talk again later,' he said, 'first you must rest.'

Obediently, Tal lay down on the rug. He felt too excited to sleep: with Argalna possibly so close at hand, it seemed such a waste of time. Yet the moment he rested his head on the soft fabric, he dropped immediately into a dreamless slumber.

He was woken at dusk by Ubek. Still half asleep, he sat up and yawned.

'Here, eat this,' Ubek said, handing him a bowl of food.

He took the bowl eagerly. He was so hungry that he had almost finished before he paused to wonder what he was eating. It had a sweetish nutty flavour which he had never experienced before.

'It is the seed of the wild grass growing all around you,' Ubek said, anticipating his question. 'Here in the Grasslands it is the basic foodstuff.'

By the time Tal had emptied the bowl, the dusk had almost faded into night. Out of habit, he peered suspiciously at the darkness on the other side of the river, and again Ubek seemed to understand his unspoken question.

'There is nothing watching you from the shadows here,' he said reassuringly.

Gathering up the rug, he led Tal away from the river. They walked through the village, where the cooking fires flared brightly in the evening breeze, towards a single hut set apart from the rest and closest to the mountains. A small lamp was already burning inside and Ubek trimmed the wick so that the flame rose higher, casting a stronger light. The interior of the hut was simply and sparely furnished and would have appeared quite unremarkable except for one thing – there were bark paintings hanging all around the wall. Tal glanced at them and then back at Ubek.

'You possess the Gift,' he said.

Ubek nodded.

'These scenes have come to me over the years,' he replied, 'and most of them I have understood. But recently I have made paintings that are a mystery to me. Look over there.'

He raised the lamp, allowing the light to shine fully on a single painting. Tal recognized the scene immediately. It was one he himself had painted: a clearing in the Greenlands; a circle of armed hunters; and a Feln charging a blurred, indistinct figure at the edge of the circle.

'The mystery is easily explained,' Tal said. 'The Feln was not really attacking the hunters. She charged at me' – he pointed to the blurred figure – 'because she sensed I would not try to kill her. She in turn spared my life.'

'I see,' Ubek said and moved the light to another painting.

Again Tal recognized the scene: the moonlit waterfall; the dark pool below; a figure falling backwards, separated from a mass of threatening black shadow only by a single stroke of gold paint.

'It is where I received this wound,' Tal explained, touching his forehead. 'Shadroth struck at me, but the Feln leaped between us and saved me.'

He ran his finger along the line of gold to show what he meant.

'Yes, I understand now,' Ubek said. 'But tell me, can you read the future as well as the past?'

He moved the lamp once again and revealed three small paintings which were more indistinct than the others. Yet despite their blurred, uncertain quality, Tal identified himself easily enough. In one, he was standing on a rocky path; in another, he seemed to be waiting in the mouth of a huge cave; and in the third, he was scrambling up through the branches of a tree. In each of the paintings an ominous black shadow stained the foreground.

'These are also of me,' Tal said, 'but I don't understand them. Nor do I understand why you have painted only these shadows. Why not Shadroth himself? He is always present.'

'Only a fool paints Shadroth,' Ubek said sharply. 'His own likeness gives him shape and form. I painted him once, long ago. I have learned my lesson now.'

Before Tal could ask him what he meant, he went on:

'I see that what you told us this morning is the truth: the Gentle Folk have nothing to fear from you. But still one thing puzzles me: who are you that you should visit my dreams in this way?'

'My name is Tal. I am the son of Norn and Erin, who died when I was an infant.'

'Ah,' Ubek breathed out, 'that explains it.'

'Explains what?' Tal asked.

Ubek replaced the lamp on the low shelf and straightened up.

'I am known by the Gentle Folk as Ubek,' he said. 'But amongst the people of the Clan, I was called Argalna.'

12. Conference

The following morning, when Tal went to see Lea, he found her awake, smiling at him in the dim interior of the hut. She was still pale and weak, but the immediate danger had passed.

'So we escaped after all,' she said in a small voice.

Tal nodded happily.

'And that's not our only good fortune,' he said. 'We've also found . . .'

But Ubek, who was standing at the foot of the bed, raised his hand, cautioning Tal to remain silent.

'We must be careful not to tire Lea with too much talk,' he said. 'Let her first regain her strength. Then will be the time for discussion.'

In her weakened state, Lea made no protest at this decision. She allowed herself to be carried outside into the warm sun where she soon fell into a light sleep.

While she slept, Tal gladly helped the Gentle Folk with their daily work. During the morning he waded through the thick waist-high grass, a woollen pouch at his side, collecting the ripe seed-heads that hung yellow and heavy from the stiff grass stems. It was a quiet, pleasant kind of labour; and it was with a sense of pride and achievement that he returned to the village at midday, his pouch filled with swollen seed-heads.

In the afternoon he was given a very different task – to accompany a group of young men and women to the foothills where they were to hunt the wild sheep. At the mention of the word hunt, Tal's eyes lit up. This was what he was used to, what he best understood. But he soon discovered that this was a very different type of hunting from anything he knew. Instead of a sling or a star-knife, he was handed nothing more dangerous than a length of twisted grass-rope lightly weighted at each end. This was whirled above the head and thrown at the sheep when they tried to escape. Tal, unpractised in the skill, flung the rope wildly in all directions, but the young people with him threw it with great accuracy, sending it coiling around the hind legs of the escaping sheep and bringing them harmlessly to the ground.

Once caught, the sheep were not butchered as they would have been in the Greenlands. They were held down only long enough for some of their wool to be plucked and then allowed to run free.

'To kill them', one young woman explained carefully, 'would benefit nobody. There would simply be one less sheep to supply us with wool.'

It was this soft springy wool, Tal learned, which was used to make the warm rugs, much of the clothing, and many other things – even the pouch which he had carried through the tall grass that morning.

By the end of the day, Tal felt that he had never enjoyed himself quite so much before. It wasn't just the work that he liked: it was the whole attitude of the people, who laughed and sang no matter what they were doing. Tal couldn't help reflecting on how different this life was from the stern, some-times harsh existence of the Clan. And as he returned from the hills in the waning light, he contemplated the coming evening with a peculiar mixture of dread and eagerness: for it was then that Ubek (as he now preferred to be called) had promised to discuss with him the grim situation in the Greenlands.

The discussion itself took place in Lea's hut. She was still too weak to stand but, having learned of Ubek's true identity, she had insisted on being present at any debate. She was talking to Molani when they arrived, sitting propped up in bed, and she gave Tal a cheery grin to show him how much better she was feeling.

It was Molani who spoke first. Leaning forward on her stick in the flickering light, she said:

'You have journeyed a long and dangerous way in search of Ubek. What exactly do you want of him?'

Lea looked across at Tal and nodded, to show that for the time being he should speak for both of them.

'We have come to ask him to return to the Greenlands,' Tal said. 'He has defeated Shadroth in the past and we need his help once again.'

'You ask for a great deal,' Molani said. 'But in a matter of this kind, Ubek can speak for himself.'

Ubek, who had been standing in the background, came forward into the circle of light and sat down on one of the low stools.

'Years ago,' he said, 'when I first arrived here, I did more than just change my name. I gave up the life and ways of the Clan. As far as I was able to, I became one of the Gentle Folk.'

There was a short silence, broken only by the shrill cries of crickets in the Grasslands.

'Are you saying you cannot go back with us?' Tal asked.

'I have made a vow never to return,' Ubek said. 'But even if I were to break that vow, it would do no good. Not now.'

'How do you know that's true?' Tal asked.

'Because it isn't within my power to achieve again what I did long ago. It can be repeated by some other person, perhaps, but not by me.'

'I don't understand you,' Tal admitted.

'Then let me explain.'

He hunched forward on the stool, the poor light accentuating the heavy lines on his face. His expression, Tal noticed, was touched with sadness, as though he were reawakening memories of a long-forgotten grief.

'Before you were born,' he said, his voice low and restrained, 'I lived in the cave dwellings of the Clan. Your father and I had been friends since childhood. We were never apart: we played together; we learned to hunt together. And by early manhood we were the greatest hunters in the Clan.

'To begin with, we entered the Greenlands only in search of food; but gradually the fever to hunt possessed us, blotting out every other concern. We were never happy unless we were tracking in the Greenlands, and no living creature was safe from us. We pursued everything, from the smallest lizard to the great-horned buck. Only the Feln escaped our attention. But not for long. In spite of the law, we soon began to imagine the excitement of hunting the huge cats. Sitting around the camp fire at night, we often talked about the beautiful coats of the Feln and what a prize they would make. Yet it wasn't really the skins which attracted us – that was merely an excuse. What lured us on was the thought that once we had killed one of the Feln, we would be undisputed lords of the Greenlands.'

'So you actually killed the Feln?' Lea broke in.

She was sitting up straight, her eyes, still slightly feverish, glittering in the lamplight.

Molani beat her stick twice on the earth floor, calling for silence.

'Hush, child,' she said, 'let him finish.'

'One day,' Ubek went on, 'we came across the tracks of a Feln. We followed them all morning and trapped the animal by the river.'

'What happened then?' Tal asked tensely.

'In that first encounter the Feln was badly wounded; but it still had strength enough to escape along the bank as far as the falls. We thought for a while we had lost it there – that it had perhaps tried to cross the river and been swept downstream. Then your father, Norn, discovered the cave behind the falls. It cannot be seen from the outside, but if you step through the light fringe of water at the very edge of the falls, it is clearly visible.

'We entered the cave, and sure enough the Feln was there: too weak now to defend itself. Even then we could have spared it, but the excitement of the hunt was upon us. So we killed it quickly and skinned it where it lay.'

Molani sighed quietly and shifted uneasily on her stool.

'The deeds of that day fill me with great shame,' Ubek admitted. 'And they are also the cause of deep regret. Because it was there, in that very cave, with the blood still fresh on our hands, that we found the charm of Shadroth. We had never seen such a thing before: it was blacker than the pool beneath the falls; sitting on a shelf at the back of the cave, as though waiting for us. And foolishly we took it with us when we left. Soon after that, Shadroth appeared in the Greenlands.'

Tal was about to interrupt with a question, but he caught Molani's warning glance and remained silent.

'We soon realized that nothing could stand against Shadroth,' Ubek continued, 'and for a time we didn't dare venture into the Greenlands after dark. During those long fearful nights we talked over the events of the past, and slowly it dawned on us that we were responsible for what had happened. That was not an easy conclusion to reach, because the charm itself exerts a power which confuses the mind of whoever wears it. But gradually we grew to understand the guilty part we had played – how we were the ones who had brought the evil into the Greenlands; how we had conjured Shadroth into being by our own senseless act of cruelty. There seemed to us then only one possible course of action to take: we had to return the charm to the cave behind the falls. For we reasoned (rightly as it turned out) that with the charm banished from the light of day, Shadroth would steal back into the dark bowels of the earth from which he had risen.'

'And is that what you did?' Lea asked.

'It wasn't as simple as it sounds,' Ubek said. 'Shadroth is wily: he always senses any threat to himself. Whenever we ventured near the cave, he always knew beforehand. Perhaps it was the charm itself which warned him. I'm not sure. But he never failed to guess our purpose: emerging even in the daylight if he had to; slinking through the green shadows beneath the trees in order to block our path. And each time he appeared, he was more visible – less a shadow and more a physical presence.

'In the end we had to devise a plan – a desperate and dangerous plan. Norn and your mother, Erin, were to act as a kind of bait to lure him away, while I carried the charm to the cave. In part, the plan worked. I reached the cave and Shadroth's power was taken from him, but not before he had trapped and killed your parents.'

Nobody tried to interrupt Ubek now. There was a long pause during which nothing moved but their flickering shadows cast onto the surrounding wall by the lamp.

'Most of what followed, you know already,' Ubek said at last. 'I found their bodies and took them back to the Slopes. That was my last visit to the Clan. I vowed then to leave, never to return. I had proved myself unfit to dwell in the Greenlands. Here, among these people' – he reached out and touched Molani gently on the arm – 'I am protected from the destructive desires which possessed me in the past.'

Again there was a period of silence. Tal, who had been sitting with bowed head, looked up slowly. The grief and regret written clearly on Ubek's face made it unnecessary for him, Tal, to say anything further about his parents' death or those events of the past. Instead, he talked quietly about the present, recounting briefly how Kulok had killed the Feln and appeared on the Slopes wearing both the skin cloak and the forbidden charm. He concluded by saying:

'So it is Kulok who has brought Shadroth back, by breaking the law of the Greenlands, and then by taking the charm from the cave.'

But to his surprise Ubek shook his head doubtfully.

'It isn't quite as straightforward as that,' he said. 'I agree that Kulok has clearly broken the law which enjoins us to kill only for food, and not out of greed or vengeance. And in taking the charm, Kulok did raise Shadroth's spirit from the darkness. But that alone does not completely explain Shadroth's presence. If what we decided long ago is correct, he doesn't actually appear until someone has painted his likeness. It is the painting which transforms him from a disembodied spirit into a visible creature that roams the surface of the earth.'

Before he could speak, Tal recognized his own startled realization on Lea's face.

'But I'm the one who painted him!' he said in a shocked voice. 'I also possess the Gift and I included him in one of my paintings.'

'Then you are partly responsible for his presence,' Ubek said softly.

'Me!' Tal burst out. 'How can you . . . ?'

But Molani put her gnarled old fingers gently to his lips, silencing him.

'This is not your guilt alone,' she told him. 'You merely expressed the secret thoughts of all those around you. Shadroth dwells in the heart of every member of the Clan. He is the monstrous child of your violent and destructive natures. That is why we fear your people. Perhaps you understand now why the villagers were at first unwilling for you to remain with us.'

Tal nodded miserably.

'It isn't the only thing I understand,' he said. 'Lea and I wondered why Shadroth followed us all the way down the river. That too is clear. Shadroth is held to me by the bond of that painting.' He stood up. 'At this very moment he might be advancing on the Grasslands. I must leave here before I bring evil upon you as well.'

'Just a moment,' Ubek said sharply, as Tal was turning away. 'Did you say he followed you all the way downriver?'

'Yes, he was there, watching us from the shore, throughout the dark hours. For three whole nights.'

'And he never left you?'

'No.'

'Then there is more than the bond of the painting between you,' Ubek said decisively. 'Shadroth would have known you were safe from him on the river. He wouldn't have kept up such a vigil without some deeper cause. Think carefully now – is there any reason for him to hate or fear you – you especially?'

'I know he hates me,' Tal answered. 'I felt his loathing when we drifted close to the bank. But I'm not sure of the reason for it. It's true that I've escaped from him twice; and since receiving this head wound I'm no longer affected by his icy cold. But why should any of that produce such hatred?'

Ubek had also risen suddenly to his feet.

'The icy presence of Shadroth doesn't affect you?' he asked.

Tal shook his head.

'Not since the attack by the falls,' he explained. 'To kill me now, he would have to strike me down like one of the cattle on the Slopes.'

Ubek drew in a deep breath.

'But don't you see!' he exclaimed. 'That is why he followed

you down the river. You are protected by the mark which he has placed upon you. Of all the living beings in the Greenlands, you alone set a limit to his power. Isn't that cause enough for hatred? A hatred born of fear?'

As he spoke, Ubek paced restlessly around the confined space of the hut. He stopped finally by the open doorway and gazed out into the starlit night, as though searching the darkness for the terrifying shadows of his youth.

'But why should Shadroth fear me?' Tal asked doubtfully. 'What could I hope to do against his terrible strength?'

Ubek remained by the doorway, sunk in thought, and Molani answered for him:

'Shadroth fears anyone or anything that could possibly harm him,' she explained. 'Take for example his fear of the river. Without the river there would be no Grasslands, and the great forest of the Greenlands would cease to be. It is the source of all life, much as Shadroth is the source of destruction and death. He knows that as well as I. He is aware that were he to immerse himself in the river, his existence would shrivel into nothing. It is for this reason that the black charm, symbol of his power, must be replaced in the cave behind the waterfall. The curtain of water is to Shadroth like an iron door through which he cannot pass. And once cut off from the charm, he has no option but to return to the dry, lightless regions deep within the earth. For it is there, far beneath the life and movement of the Greenlands, that he truly belongs.'

Lea, who had been silent for some time, leaned forward.

'Is the replacing of the charm the only way of breaking his power?' she asked.

'It is the only sure way,' Molani replied.

'In that case there is little hope,' Lea said sadly. 'Kulok is my brother; I know him well. He has always been strong-willed; and now, with the charm in his possession, he will listen to nobody. He would only laugh if I asked him to give up the charm.'

'Nonetheless, you must still ask him,' Molani advised.

'Yes, we will,' Lea agreed, 'but I fear it will do no good. I wish there were another way.'

'There may be,' Ubek said suddenly, his voice unexpectedly loud in the confined space of the hut.

He moved abruptly away from the doorway and came back into the circle of light. Although he had seemed to be answering Lea, his eyes were fixed on Tal.

'Explain yourself, Ubek,' Molani said quietly.

He nodded, still without taking his eyes from Tal.

'Nobody has ever been able to test Shadroth's true strength, because it has been impossible to approach him. The coldness of his presence withers the life of even the bravest warriors. But now the situation is different: this boy can live and breathe in that icy atmosphere.'

'What are you suggesting?' Molani asked in a worried voice.

'Always, in the past,' Ubek said, 'Shadroth has been the hunter. Never has he been one of the hunted. The time has come for that to change.'

Molani also stood up, slowly and stiffly, and put an arm protectively around Tal's shoulders.

'But he is not yet a man,' she protested, holding Tal close against her.

'He possesses something more important than the strength of manhood,' Ubek countered. 'He can survive the deadening presence of Shadroth.'

'And do you think that's protection enough?' Lea broke in. She was staring at Ubek, a look of disbelief in her eyes.

'Perhaps Tal himself should be the judge of that,' he replied.

Tal pulled gently free of Molani and stood before Ubek.

'What exactly are you asking of me?' he said.

But it was an unnecessary question, because he already knew the answer.

'I am asking whether you will undertake the hunting of Shadroth,' Ubek said.

13. Return

During the two weeks it took for Lea to regain her strength there were many more discussions about the evil situation in the Greenlands; but nothing new was added to the original debate. Ubek remained firmly convinced that Shadroth must be hunted down and destroyed; while Molani repeated her claim that such a venture was far too dangerous, and probably impossible.

'You are sending the boy to his death,' she argued. 'Kulok possesses the charm and only he can banish the evil.'

'Then why does Shadroth hate and fear the boy?' Ubek objected. 'Isn't it proof that Tal poses a threat to him?'

Tal himself took very little part in these discussions. He had never actually agreed to the idea of the hunt – not because he thought Ubek was wrong, but simply because his courage failed him whenever he considered the possibility of setting out to destroy Shadroth. He preferred to put such terrifying suggestions completely out of his mind. With Lea still too weak to travel, it was easier to ignore the future – especially with so much to occupy him during the day.

From first light until dusk he was busy roaming the Grasslands or tracking the wild sheep in the foothills. Every evening, tired and happy, he would return from the mountains with a band of young people. In the growing dusk they would trot contentedly along the narrow paths that cut through the tall grass, singing together the ancient lilting songs of the Gentle Folk. Always, before entering the village, they would plunge into the shallows of the river, laughing and shouting as they swam or splashed each other, enjoying the pleasant coolness of the water which washed away the dust and fatigue of the day.

After the ordeal of his recent journey and the shame and

misery of those final weeks on the Slopes, rejected and abused by most of the Clan, his life amongst the Gentle Folk was like a whole new beginning. He understood completely why Ubek had lost all desire to return to the Clan. He, too, would have liked to forget the challenge that awaited him in the Greenlands. It was so much more pleasant to remain where he was, caught up in the peaceful, unchallenging life of the village.

Yet although he tried to put all thought of the future completely out of mind, he couldn't totally ignore the fact that Lea was growing steadily stronger. One evening when he returned, she was waiting for him down by the river. There was a warm healthy glow in her cheeks which told him far more clearly than words that the time had come for a decision. They stood facing each other for several moments without speaking.

'There's no reason for delaying any longer,' Lea said quietly. 'The longer we remain here, the more of a physical presence Shadroth will become.'

He turned and looked at the dark forbidding outline of the mountains.

'What's the good of going back at all?' he said, shuffling his feet uncomfortably. 'We can't do any good there.'

'We can at least ask Kulok to give up the charm,' she said.

'Do you think that will achieve anything?'

'No, but Molani is right: we have to speak to him just the same. Nobody else in the Greenlands understands the power of the charm or what has to be done with it.'

Tal wanted to ask her what they would do after they'd spoken to Kulok; but as always he lacked the courage to voice his deepest fears. Instead, he silently nodded his agreement and walked slowly back towards the huts.

The whole village came out to see them off the following morning. They were much better equipped now than when they had arrived. Each of them carried a light pack in which there were flints for making fire, warm woollen rugs, and a plentiful supply of dried grain. As the sun rose beyond the river, Ubek and Molani escorted them as far as a fork in the path which led out of the village.

'Are you sure you won't return with us?' Lea asked Ubek hopefully.

It was the same question they had put to him many times before, and he shook his head sadly.

'Even were I to accompany you, I could give you little help. You now know as much about Shadroth as I do: it is for you and Kulok to decide the future of the Clan.'

He stepped back as Molani placed her hand on each of their heads in turn, blessing them.

'Go safely,' she said, 'and may the spirit of peace guide you on your journey.'

She paused, leaning heavily on her stick, then fixed Tal with her eyes.

'If you ever take Ubek's advice,' she said, 'and decide to face Shadroth, remember this – remember it well, for your life will depend upon it. No living creature can hope to defeat Shadroth. If Shadroth is to be destroyed, it must be by himself. He alone possesses the necessary power.'

Tal and Lea both looked puzzled by her words.

'But how can anyone persuade Shadroth to destroy himself?' Tal asked.

'The Gentle Folk cannot tell you how to hunt,' Molani said softly. 'We can only tell you the truth as we see it. The rest is for you to decide.'

There was a finality about her tone which prevented Tal from asking any further questions; and after thanking the old woman and Ubek, they turned and took the narrower of the two paths through the wind-blown grass.

As Molani had told them it would, this path slanted towards the foothills and then turned and followed the curving line of the mountain chain. They travelled along it for five whole days. At night they built a small fire on which to roast the dry grain they had brought with them; and as there was little shelter to be had, they slept out in the open. This was no hardship: the nights were warm, and to protect themselves from the stony ground they gathered great bundles of the wild thyme which grew all over the otherwise bare hillsides.

Throughout that part of their journey, nothing occurred

either to delay them or to disturb their rest at night. On several occasions they saw villages belonging to the Gentle Folk, but they were always far in the distance, clusters of tiny brown dots surrounded by a sea of grass. They toiled on along the dusty path, pausing only for short rests; and with every passing mile the mountains on their right grew steadily higher, so that each morning it took a little longer for the sun to appear above the craggy peaks. By the fifth day the towering heights above them had taken on the familiar outline which they had known all their lives; and that afternoon the path began to zigzag upwards, towards a narrow steep-sided pass which looked as though it had been cut out of the living rock with a giant knife.

That night they camped just below the pass. At such a high altitude there was a frosty bite to the air; and the cold, plus the thought of what lay beyond the mountains, destroyed their earlier feeling of security. Molani had told them that Shadroth would not venture west of the pass into the domain of the Gentle Folk; but despite this knowledge, they found it difficult to sleep.

Most of the night they dozed before the fire, wrapped in the soft rugs they had brought with them. At one point, during the early hours, Tal became fully awake and looked up towards the pass. Just for a moment a black shadow seemed to move across the opening. He glanced quickly away and edged closer to the fire. He told himself that what he had seen was no more than a cloud passing before the sliver of moon, but for the remainder of the night he found it more difficult than ever to relax.

The dawn came as a welcome relief to both of them. They were cold and stiff as well as nervous, and in the first grey light of morning they shouldered their packs and resumed their climb up through the frosty air. The sun had just risen when they reached the pass, and they paused for a moment or two, enjoying the feel of the warm sunlight on their faces. Spread out below them was the Greenlands, the vast plain divided evenly in two by the Broad River. In the far distance they could see the sheer sandstone cliffs in the base of which the Clan had excavated their homes.

'Aren't you glad to be back?' Lea said happily.

He looked out over the huge expanse which he had once loved so much and nodded half-heartedly. In the clear yellow sunlight the Greenlands was a pool of vivid sparkling green beneath the pale blue of the morning sky. Yet after his experience at the falls, Tal could see it only as a dark and gloomy place. To his troubled gaze, its very vastness posed a hidden threat which he instinctively flinched from. He would have liked nothing better than to retreat to the safety of the Grasslands once again. Had he been alone, he might even have done so. But he was conscious of Lea beside him, watching him, and with a determined shrug of the shoulders he hitched his pack a little higher and stepped forward onto the downward slope.

The steep descent was both long and hazardous, and as they hoped to reach the safety of the falls before nightfall, there was no time to stop and rest. For hour after hour, they clambered or slithered down the rocky path. On either side of them the barren hillsides were a blinding white in the hot sunlight. Nothing moved or grew anywhere on those arid slopes and the only sound in the deathly stillness was that of their own sliding footsteps. It was impossible even to talk together because the path was too narrow for them to travel side by side. One behind the other, they toiled downwards through the growing heat of the day, enveloped in a haze of powdery dust that was kicked up by their feet.

Yet although they were soon hot and tired, they continued to keep a sharp watch on their surroundings. Whenever it was safe to do so, they looked around them, searching the rocky slopes. Their vigilance was rewarded early in the afternoon. By then they were only a mile or two from the edge of the Greenlands and the path had levelled out considerably. They came around a sharp bend and there, clearly visible in the bare hillside, was the entrance to a cave.

Ubek had told them about the cave before they left the village, suggesting it as a place in which they could shelter from Shadroth. The entrance, as they could now see, was hardly large enough to admit a fully grown man or woman; it would have been impossible for Shadroth to squeeze his huge bulk into so small an opening.

Slipping off their packs, they crawled inside and inched their way along a tunnel which ran for six or seven feet before it opened up into a larger cavern. Satisfied that the cave would offer adequate protection if they needed it, they re-emerged into the sunlight and prepared to continue their journey. But just as Tal was lifting his pack, he noticed something else which made him pause.

'Look!' he said, pointing over to the right.

Some distance away, and considerably above the level on which they stood, was what appeared to be a broad, raised path or causeway which led directly to the mouth of a far larger cave. There was something about that dark opening which told him clearly what it meant. And if there had been any doubt in his mind it was immediately dispelled by his memory of one of Ubek's paintings. In the painting, he had been standing on a causeway just like this one, with an ominous black shadow darkening the ground before him.

'What is it?' Lea asked.

'It is Shadroth's lair,' he said quietly.

The mere mention of such a place brought a chill into the heat of the day, and without another word they hurried on their way.

It was as well that they did. Neither of them knew this portion of the Greenlands very well and they wasted a considerable amount of time battling through the heavy undergrowth in their search for a path which led in the right direction. When, eventually, they found one, the afternoon was already well advanced. And it was early evening before they reached the river.

In the rapidly fading light they ran towards the booming sound of the falls. Only the top half of the sun was showing above the mountains, and that too slid out of sight as they skirted the deep pool. With the shadows darkening around them, they walked carefully out across the slippery shelf of rock and edged thankfully behind the protective curtain of falling water.

After the warm muggy atmosphere of the outside, the interior of the cave struck cold on their bare skin. The unexpected cold, plus the deep gloom, made them pause and instinctively draw back. As they did so, something stirred in the depths of the cave and began to glide menacingly towards them. It all happened so suddenly, just when they thought they were safe, that for a moment or two neither of them could move. It was as if Ubek's warning had been in vain and they had come all this way only to walk into a trap – Shadroth's ghostly presence waiting for them even here, where they had hoped to find sanctuary.

Lea was the first to realize their mistake.

'Tal!' she said excitedly, 'it's the Feln!'

She was right: there before them was the familiar golden-coated creature – the same animal that had followed them down the river. Lea, relieved as well as pleased, ran forward and threw her arms affectionately around the Feln's powerful neck.

'You see!' she cried triumphantly. 'She knew we'd return. She's been waiting here for us.'

But Tal didn't reply. The shock which he'd just experienced seemed to have jarred something alive in his head. He was no longer looking at Lea and the Feln. Momentarily, the Gift possessed him, and he could see nothing but the picture in his own mind. It was a picture of himself. He was standing in some kind of high-ceilinged place that was lit by flares, and he was facing Shadroth. But that wasn't all: in this particular picture, he was huge, as tall and powerful as the evil shape which confronted him – he and Shadroth, like two giant beings, preparing to fight to the death.

It was Lea's voice, calling to him, which dissolved the picture.

'Tal!' she said urgently. 'What's the matter?'

His eyes cleared and he heard again the crashing of the falls behind him.

'Something was happening to you,' she said. 'What was it?'

He shook his head.

'Nothing,' he said, 'nothing.'

14. Seeds of Destruction

Piles of driftwood littered the floor of the cave, washed in there some time in the past when the river had been in flood. Using the flints given them by the Gentle Folk, Lea and Tal lit a small fire to comfort as well as to warm them in the chill atmosphere. By its flickering light, they could see at the far end of the cave the broad shelf from which the black charm had been taken. Even now, with the charm gone, there appeared to be a gloomy, almost brooding quality about the area around the shelf, and they kept well away from it.

Sitting close to the fire, with the Feln blinking sleepily between them, they talked about their journey – having to raise their voices above the constant roar of the falls.

'What amazes me,' Tal said, 'is the way the Feln knew we would come here and was already waiting for us.'

'It's not really surprising,' Lea answered. 'This is where it all began: where her mate was killed and the charm was stolen by Kulok. If Ubek and Molani are right, it's also where the trouble must end. Looked at in that way, it's the most obvious place for her to come.'

'Yes, I suppose so,' Tal agreed. 'But it still puzzles me that the Feln are so important in this whole business.'

'I talked about that to Molani,' Lea replied. 'She says the Feln are the true lords of the Greenlands, not Kulok or the elders or anybody else. Take the way they kill only for food, for instance – that's a sort of rule which no other creature ought to disobey; it's what makes the Greenlands the place it is, the place we love. Occasionally, members of the Clan break that rule, when they kill one of the Feln. They shouldn't, but they do. It's a senseless act of destruction which changes the Greenlands, makes it different. And it's then that Shadroth rises, because he's the spirit of destruction. That's all he is, according to Molani. He's a kind of living proof of what people actually think or feel.'

'And do you think the Feln understand all this?' Tal asked.

Lea shrugged.

'I don't know. All I'm sure about is that they see Shadroth as their enemy.'

'But Shadroth is everyone's enemy,' Tal said. 'Even Kulok would probably be destroyed if he remained unprotected in the Greenlands after dark.'

'Yes, but Shadroth is the Feln's particular enemy,' Lea insisted. 'They're kinds of opposites – like life and death, or light and darkness. Molani says that defeating Shadroth and protecting the Feln are really the same thing, and I agree with her.'

While they talked, the Feln lay sprawled out before the fire, apparently unaware that she was being discussed. She showed no sign of following anything Lea was saying – yet still the fact remained that she had come there and waited for them; and if Shadroth had suddenly appeared in the vicinity, she would have been instantly on the alert, ready to protect them with her life if necessary – Tal had discovered that during the incident at the falls. Such considerations, he had to admit, made sense of Molani's ideas. It was as if the Feln understood that although the people of the Clan had threatened her and killed her mate, there was nothing to be gained by attacking them. She seemed to have grasped the notion that the only hope for the Greenlands lay in her combining with members of the Clan to defeat the common enemy.

Like the Feln, Tal and Lea also lay down to sleep soon afterwards. Ubek had assured them that Shadroth hated and feared the cave behind the falls, much as any other creature might fear a cage or prison, and would not go near it unless he had to. With that knowledge to comfort them, they slept far more peacefully than they had on the previous night. Tal was woken only once, by the throbbing of the wound in his forehead. But the pain was not intense, which meant Shadroth was some distance away, nor did it last very long. After throwing another

117

log on the fire, he lay down once again and soon drifted back into a restful sleep.

They awoke next morning feeling completely refreshed. Before the sun had risen, they had left the cave and, with the Feln close behind them, were hurrying along the paths which led towards the Slopes. They had a particular reason for their early start. Their immediate aim was to find Kulok and plead with him to give up the charm. But if he refused to agree, which was what they feared, there still had to be time enough to return to the falls before nightfall.

As they ran along the green sun-speckled paths, Lea frequently looked back at Tal and grinned, conveying the pleasure she felt at being in familiar surroundings. But he still found it difficult to respond to her cheerfulness. An atmosphere of gloom and foreboding seemed to cling to everything – to the trees and coiling mass of vines with their bright delicate flowers, even to the bird and animal life.

Their present venture did nothing to relieve this gloomy feeling. They had decided that when they reached the Slopes, Tal and the Feln should wait in the cover of the Greenlands while Lea went up to the cave dwellings alone. Whatever else Kulok might do, there was little chance that he would threaten the life of his own sister. But if she hadn't returned within an hour, Tal should assume that she was being held prisoner by the Clan and return to the falls without her. That possibility, the thought of losing Lea's courage and companionship, made him feel sadder and more discouraged than ever.

Yet as things turned out, they never had a chance to put their plan into action. It was mid morning and they were travelling along a broad path which was completely shaded by the thick canopy above. Tal, ever on the alert when he was in the Greenlands, suddenly heard an unusual sound up ahead and signalled for Lea to stop. The Feln, who had also heard it, growled deep in her throat. Quickly, they stepped off the path and crouched, hidden, in the undergrowth.

Less than a minute later, a band of hunters appeared around a bend in the path. They were walking two abreast and Kulok himself was leading them. As always, the black charm hung at his throat, and draped around his shoulders was the golden cloak. But now he wasn't the only man who owned one: no fewer than five of the other hunters wore them. Again the Feln growled, more in anger than warning, and Tal placed a hand on her neck to quieten her – his fingers instinctively seeking out the ridge of scar which was like a bond between them.

Indicating that Tal should remain in hiding, Lea stood up and faced the advancing hunters. Kulok stopped in mid-stride, while behind him the hunters cried out in surprise.

'She lives!' someone said in an awed whisper. 'Shadroth has not taken her!'

For a moment it seemed that Kulok was going to rush forward and embrace her; but he held himself back, the look of welcome quickly masked, giving way to his habitually stern expression.

'Are you also in league with Shadroth?' he asked sharply.

'I come not from Shadroth,' she answered, 'but from Argalna, the greatest hunter in the history of the Clan.'

'Argalna is dead,' Kulok said.

'No,' Lea said firmly, 'he is still alive and he sends a message to you.'

There were murmurs of curiosity from the hunters who had crowded forward on the narrow path.

'He says there are two things you have to do,' Lea went on. 'You must stop hunting the Feln; and you must return the black charm to the place where you found it – to the cave behind the falls. Only then will Shadroth leave us.'

The effect of her words on Kulok surprised even Tal. The young chieftain hastily drew back, both hands raised to his throat, as though to protect the charm which nestled there.

'How can a mere trinket affect the will of Shadroth?' Kulok said, unable to keep the alarm out of his voice. 'This is just a trick! You haven't even seen Argalna!'

'Why should I wish to trick you?' Lea asked.

'Because it is easier than answering the obvious charge against you,' Kulok said deliberately. 'You have survived here in the Greenlands for many weeks. How is such a thing possible without the aid of Shadroth?'

'Do you dare to ask me that when you wear Shadroth's emblem at your throat?' Lea cried. 'It is you who must answer for your actions, not me!'

A dark frown of anger creased Kulok's forehead.

'I am not interested in arguing with you,' he said. 'You will accompany us back to the Slopes. We will see what the people think of your childish lies about Argalna.'

He stepped aside, intending two of the hunters to go forward and seize her, but at that moment Tal and the Feln rose from their hiding place and moved protectively to her side.

Again there were cries of surprise, mingled now with sounds of fear and horror. It wasn't only the sudden appearance of the Feln which alarmed them, but also the black wound, like a fragment of night, which showed clearly on Tal's forehead. Kulok was one of the first to recover.

'I see,' he said bitterly, speaking to Lea. 'You have chosen this outcast rather than your own people. You prefer an enemy of the Clan, one who now wears Shadroth's mark upon him for all to witness. He has become a thing of darkness and evil and must pay the price – and so must you if you remain with him.'

As he spoke, Kulok slowly brought his shield up before him, his right hand groping furtively for the star-knife wedged inside the circle of hardened leather. But Tal was ready for such a move. While he and the Feln had lain hidden beside the path, he had unlooped his sling and loaded it with one of the heavier stones from his pouch. Now, at the first sign of the star-knife being drawn from the shield, Tal whirled the sling and shot the stone directly at Kulok.

He intended it to hit him only on the chest, as on that earlier occasion when they had confronted each other. But in his haste he aimed slightly too high, and the stone flew straight at Kulok's throat, to the exact spot where the charm now hung. Caught unawares, Kulok was too late in throwing up his shield. There was a sharp crack as the stone struck the black image and glanced off, and in that very instant the whole of the Greenlands seemed to shudder and sway. The ground shook beneath their feet; the sunlight dimmed, as though the day were about to be engulfed by night; an icy gale of wind swept through the surrounding trees, tearing off branches and forcing the hunters to their knees. But worst of all was the distant cry. It came from the barren hillside beyond the river: a terrible piercing shriek that rang out over the Greenlands – not the death call which Tal had heard before, but a scream of pure anguish, a cry of blind agonizing torment which echoed from one side of the plain to the other.

After it had died away, nothing stirred. There was complete silence. It took several minutes for the strong sunlight to dispel the darkness and for the normal sounds of the Greenlands to return. Slowly, one by one, the hunters picked themselves up, glancing fearfully around them, as though expecting Shadroth to come crashing through the trees in the wake of his terrible cry. But for the moment the terror had passed. Only Kulok had not risen: he remained stretched out on the ground, his eyes wide open, staring blankly into space. His men helped him to his feet, but still it was some time before he understood where he was. He appeared changed, smaller somehow, almost shrunken, and in place of his stern, arrogant attitude, he now wore an expression of fear and bewilderment.

'Where have they gone?' he said in a frightened voice.

The other hunters didn't realize what he meant at first.

'Lea and Tal,' he said, 'where are they? It's not safe for them to be left alone in the Greenlands. Shadroth will destroy them.'

Two of the hunters ran off, only to return soon afterwards with the news that there was no sign of them.

'But they have to be found!' Kulok said urgently. 'We can't leave them here after dark. We must split up and search as far as the river.'

Several of the men, mystified by his sudden shift of attitude, exchanged glances.

'We are here to hunt the Feln,' someone murmured.

'No!' Kulok said firmly. 'We will have no more hunting of the Feln. Not while I am chieftain.'

There was, as he said these words, a look of regret and longing in his eyes. It was exactly as if he had suddenly woken from a trance-like state – as if Shadroth's cry of anguish had severed some invisible chain which had bound him to the darkness. And now, at last, he was himself again.

But unfortunately for Tal and Lea, they knew nothing of this. While the hunters had been sprawled out on the ground, they had turned and run back down the trail. They didn't slacken their pace until they had put several miles between themselves and Kulok; and they didn't stop and rest until they had reached the river. For the remainder of the day, still in the company of the Feln, they crouched in the shallows, completely hidden by the thick margin of reeds which lined the bank. More than once in the early afternoon, they heard hunters moving along the near-by paths. But nobody came close enough to see them; and as the day wore on, those occasional sounds of pursuit also disappeared.

They didn't emerge into the open until shortly before dark. With the last of the sunlight streaking the tops of the trees, they ran upriver and again slipped behind the falls into the security of the cave. There were no indications that anybody had visited the cave in their absence, and that was a relief to both of them. For Lea, it was the only bright spot in the whole day. Everything else seemed nothing short of disastrous, a mere waste of time and effort.

Yet for once Tal did not share her view. He, more than anyone else, had recognized the note of deep anguish in Shadroth's cry – mainly because it had echoed his own experience that night beside the falls, when the tip of the claw had entered his forehead. What that distant cry had told him was that Shadroth was vulnerable: he was not all-powerful; he, too, like every other creature, could be scared and hurt.

Throughout the afternoon, as he crouched amongst the reeds, Tal thought carefully about this new and vital discovery; and by evening the first vague suggestion of an idea had begun to form in his mind. He didn't yet possess what could truly be called a plan of action; but a sixth sense told him that at least he was beginning to think in the right kind of way – that hidden somewhere in Shadroth's tormented scream lay the seeds of his ultimate destruction.

PART III · THE HUNT BEGINS

15. Shadroth's Lair

They didn't discuss the strange events of that day until after they had lit a fire and eaten their evening meal. Only then did Lea ask a question which had been puzzling her ever since their encounter with Kulok.

'That cry we heard today,' she said, as they sat before the brightly burning logs, 'what did it mean? Have you any idea?'

'It was a cry of pain,' Tal answered. 'I'm certain of that.'

Lea nodded in agreement.

'Yes,' she said, 'that's what I thought. I couldn't work it out at first – you know, the idea of the charm hurting him when he was so far away. But then I remembered what Argalna and Molani told us, and it all became depressingly clear.'

Her voice was unusually sad and subdued, and at that moment she looked as miserable as she sounded.

'Why should their words depress you?' Tal asked.

'Because Shadroth's scream of pain proved that what they told us is true: the charm is the only sure way of striking at him. Whether we want to imprison him deep within the earth where he belongs or simply inflict pain on him, it has to be through the charm. And Kulok made it obvious that he won't give it up.'

Tal stared silently into the fire for some time before replying.

'I agree that the charm does seem to exert some power over Shadroth,' he said at last, 'but does that mean it's the only way of striking at him? Couldn't there be other ways?'

Lea looked up quickly.

'Can you suggest anything else?' she asked.

'I'm not sure,' Tal admitted. 'I've been thinking about it all afternoon, and Molani's closing words to us keep coming back to me. Do you remember what she said: how Shadroth can be destroyed only by himself?'

'Yes,' Lea said, 'but I didn't understand her.'

'Nor did I. Not until today. But this afternoon, when we were hiding in the reeds, her advice suddenly began to make sense. You see, the charm is a miniature version of Shadroth – it has the same blackness, the same two glowing points of eyes. In a sense, it's a part of him. And that's why it can be used to destroy him. When the charm is banished from the light and air and freedom of the Greenlands, so too is Shadroth.'

'You may be right,' Lea said. 'Even so, how does it help us? We're still left with the fact that Kulok refuses to give up the charm.'

'But don't you see!' Tal insisted. 'If we're right, then other things could be used against him just as successfully. There's nothing unique about the charm. Anything else would do, as long as it belongs to him. That's the important point – to have power over him, it has to be some portion of himself. I think that's what Molani meant.'

Lea still appeared slightly puzzled.

'What do you mean by a portion of himself?' she said.

Tal rummaged in his leather pouch and brought out the fragment of claw which had once been lodged in his forehead. It was as black as ever and, although it was tiny, it had about it the same sinister quality as the charm.

'This is probably too small,' he said, 'but if we could get a bigger piece, the whole claw perhaps, we might be able to use it against him.'

'You think it would be more effective than an ordinary sling or star-knife?' Lea asked.

'I've already proved that they're useless,' Tal said. 'The night Galt died, I used my sling as I did today – except that I shot the stone at Shadroth himself. I'm fairly certain of that. And it had no effect. I heard it strike him, and I felt the cold gust of his anger, but that was all.'

Lea stood up and walked thoughtfully over to the far wall of the cave. She stood there for several seconds before she turned and came slowly back. The doubt in her mind was clearly written on her face.

'You don't believe I'm right, do you?' he said, disappointed.

'I can't make up my mind,' she admitted. 'For all I know, your theory may be correct: it might be possible to use Shadroth's own weapons against him. But still that isn't quite what Molani said. It was Shadroth's *power* that she spoke of. How did she put it? – Shadroth has to destroy himself. Surely if she'd meant things like claws, she would have said so.'

'You think we'd be wasting our time, then?' Tal said.

'Yes, we probably would,' she replied.

Yet in spite of her answer, she continued to pace restlessly up and down, as though she were still struggling to make up her mind about what had been said.

'In that case,' Tal murmured, 'there's nothing else we can do except sit here and wait.'

He was speaking more to himself than to Lea, but his words had a decided effect on her. She stopped her pacing and came back to the fire.

'No,' she said firmly, 'anything is better than just sitting here. Let's give your idea a try. At least that way we'll discover the truth. What do you suggest we do first?'

It was the one question he had been dreading all along; and to delay answering, he picked up a piece of stick and poked at the fire with it.

'You must have worked something out,' she said encouragingly.

Behind them, the river continued to crash noisily over the falls, forming a protective curtain between them and the night. There, in the security of the cave, it was hard for him to contemplate going out into the darkness. Yet what he had to suggest was worse even than that.

'There's only one possible course of action as far as I can see,' he said, 'and it would be extremely dangerous.'

Lea came and crouched beside him, the two of them hunched forward over the fire. It was as if they were trying to keep back unpleasant memories of a cold night wind.

'You mean go up to that cave, to his lair, and search?' Lea asked.

'What other way is there?' he said softly. 'That's the trouble with the whole idea. I don't see how we could ever survive, even in daylight.'

'Then why not go at night,' Lea said, 'while Shadroth is away?'

'What if he returned?'

Lea stood up abruptly and went round to the other side of the fire. The light from the flames made her face appear unusually flushed, alive with excitement.

'He wouldn't return if he was busy elsewhere,' she said. 'If I were to go downriver and lure him away, you'd be free to search his lair. Provided you were well clear before dawn, you'd be safe. You could take shelter in that cave we found beside the path; and we could meet back here later in the morning.'

'You seem to forget that my parents died trying to lure Shadroth away,' Tal reminded her.

'I know that,' Lea replied gently. 'But I wouldn't take any unnecessary chances, I promise. I could carry the two rugs with me: they'd provide some protection from the cold. And I wouldn't stray far from the river. Under those circumstances, I'd probably be safer than you, up there in the hills alone.'

Now it was Tal's turn to hesitate.

'We'd both be taking a terrible risk,' he said evasively.

'That's true enough,' Lea conceded. 'But what choice do we have? This is the one opportunity left to us of defeating Shadroth. We have to take it.'

Tal had no ready answer to such an argument. Secretly, he knew that Lea was only voicing what was already at the back of his own mind. He didn't admit that openly – and he continued to argue with her until deep into the night. Yet when they finally lay down to sleep, there was a silent understanding between them. The time for cowering in the safety of the cave had passed.

They slept late the next morning, and then, for several hours, they gathered fruit and berries on the western side of the river – where there was less likelihood of being seen by members of the Clan. Neither of them spoke very much about their decision. In the middle of the afternoon, Lea simply bundled up the rugs, took a small portion of the food, and prepared to set out.

'At least take the Feln with you,' Tal said. 'She guided me safely when I was running from Shadroth.'

'The Feln will probably make her own choice,' Lea replied, 'just the same as we have.'

She walked over to the entrance of the cave and paused for a moment, looking back at the huge cat sprawled out on the floor beside Tal. The Feln yawned and turned her head away, showing no inclination to follow.

'It seems she's already made up her mind,' Lea said.

And before Tal could wave or wish her good luck, she stepped around the curtain of water and disappeared.

They had agreed earlier that Tal should not set out until after dark, when Shadroth would already have left his lair. This meant that he had nothing to do in the meantime but sit and wait. It was, for him, the worst time of all. To while away the hours, he tried recalling other, happier times; but despite his efforts, he found it impossible to forget even for a moment the ordeal which awaited him up in the hills. He kept asking himself the same question over and over – would he have the strength of will to carry out his part of the plan and actually enter the dark mouth of that distant cave?

Nor was that fear the only thing which worried him. Other considerations persistently crowded into his mind. There was the vision he had had, when the Gift had possessed him, in which he and Shadroth faced each other. Would that happen tonight? And if so, how would he take on the giant proportions of that figure in the vision? Or had his unnatural size been little more than a trick of the light?

Where Shadroth was concerned, nothing seemed certain. Why, for example, had he not bothered them for the past twenty-four hours? After the incident with Kulok and the scream of torment which had issued from the hills, Tal had taken it for granted that Shadroth would haunt the vicinity of the falls, breathing out his cold hatred and desire for revenge. Yet they had slept undisturbed throughout the previous night. Not once had the throbbing pain in Tal's forehead signalled the evil presence. It just didn't make sense – that Shadroth should follow them all the way downriver, and then, when he had a genuine reason for revenge, not come near them. Unless, of course, that scream had been his own death cry and he was stark and still up there in the hills. For a few minutes, Tal toyed hopefully with that idea. But it was too much to expect – Tal realized that – and he soon reverted to his former anxious thoughts.

When the long dark shadows finally began to enter the cave, he felt almost relieved. Anything was better than sitting there with nothing to do but worry. In the gathering dusk, he stood just inside the foaming curtain of water, impatient to be off; and as soon as the sky was black directly above him, he slipped out into the warm dark world of the Greenlands.

Like Lea, he made no effort to coax the Feln, but when he glanced over his shoulder she was there behind him, padding silently along the dim path. She followed him for some time, and then, as if sensing their ultimate destination, brushed past him and led the way. He was glad of that: the Greenlands, by night, were more gloomy and threatening than ever; every moving shadow or rustling of the trees made him catch his breath in alarm, and it was comforting to have the Feln there in front of him, like a physical barrier protecting him from whatever might lurk in their path.

With the Feln leading them by the shortest route, they soon reached the edge of the Greenlands. Above them rose the barren slopes of the foothills, and beyond those the craggy peaks of the mountain chain. A thin moon had risen, casting just enough light to bring out the ghostly whiteness of the bare rocky hillsides.

The Feln had already left the cover of the Greenlands and was standing out in the open, her golden coat glowing faintly in the darkness. Tal remained in the deep shade of the trees for several minutes longer, unwilling to venture out until he was quite sure that it was safe to do so. His eyes and ears searched the night for unfamiliar or warning sounds. But all was calm and still, and cautiously he, too, emerged into the open.

From that point on, there was very little cover for them. If Shadroth was anywhere near, his gleaming red eyes, able to pierce the blackest night, would already be following their progress across the bare slopes. That possibility was never far from Tal's mind and even the slightest change in his surroundings sent warning shocks of fear through him. Once, when a bank of cloud sailed across the face of the moon, he was so startled that he could not prevent himself from crying out in fright. But in spite of his nervousness, the Feln appeared completely unperturbed. She bounded on ahead of him, slowing down or stopping only when he fell too far behind.

Instead of taking him straight up the path towards the pass, she led him across the hillside to a steeper, narrower track that zigzagged up to the raised causeway he had seen two days earlier. The causeway itself was wider than he had imagined it – like a broad highway thrusting out from the mountainside, the ground falling sharply away on either side. Once on this highway, even the Feln slowed down: with her ears flattened close to her head, she moved cautiously forward, stopping frequently to scent the breeze which blew gently towards them. She knew as well as Tal that if they were caught up there, escape would not be easy, perhaps impossible: the sides of the causeway were so steep they were almost vertical; and now that the moon was completely obscured by cloud, Shadroth would have an advantage over them.

And yet, to Tal's amazement and relief, there was still no sign of that chilling presence. The light wind blowing into their faces remained as pleasantly warm as ever; and the wound in his forehead gave no warning of danger. Groping their way slowly forward in the darkness, they came at last to the huge cave. It loomed up before them like a gaping black mouth, waiting to devour whoever dared to enter. Against the ghostly grey-white of the dry rock-strewn hillside, it showed as a rough circle of deepest night. For the first time since leaving the safety of the falls, the Feln growled angrily: crouched low, her body turned sideways to the cave, she seemed about to bound away down the slope. But nothing rushed out of the shadows towards them. The cave, Tal now felt sure, was empty. Kneeling down beside the Feln, he stroked the raised fur along her neck, reassuring her.

'It's all right,' he whispered softly, 'Shadroth isn't here.'

Where then, Tal wondered, was he? Could it be that he was pursuing Lea along the river? Quickly, Tal dismissed that thought from his mind and stood up.

The Feln, although quiet, was far from calm; and when he again moved forward, she remained in the background, always a few yards behind him, her yellow eyes glinting distrustfully.

'Come,' he whispered, 'there's nothing to fear.'

Those were more than just empty words of encouragement: at that moment he truly believed they were safe. But as he stepped into the mouth of the cave, his mood changed: suddenly he felt sure that he would never return along the causeway, that once inside Shadroth's lair he would be trapped.

16. Trapped

Tal was unprepared for the shock of cold which greeted him as he entered the cave. It was like stepping into the middle of the most deadening winter, and for a split second he wondered whether he had been wrong – whether perhaps Shadroth was waiting for him after all. But no, there was no death cry to accompany the icy temperature, and his footsteps echoed hollowly in the deserted cavern.

Behind him, the Feln snarled uneasily and he looked back. She had stopped in the entrance, clearly unwilling to come any further. He thought at first she was worried by the cold – and then immediately realized his mistake. There was something else about the place, something only partly disguised by the freezing atmosphere: a lingering odour of death and decay; the rank smell of rotting flesh. Involuntarily, he found himself breathing shallowly and he was almost overcome by the urge to be physically sick. Only with an effort did he manage to control his churning stomach. As he stood there panting lightly, trying not to breathe in too much of the putrefying smell, he was for the first time glad of Shadroth's ability to freeze everything he approached. The atmosphere in there was bad enough: in the warm night air the smell would have been overpowering.

Doing his best to ignore it, Tal stumbled forward in the almost total darkness until his feet kicked against some dry sticks lying on the floor. That in itself was lucky, more than he could have hoped for; and gathering up an armful of sticks, he groped his way to one of the side walls, where he could not be seen from outside. He had brought with him the flints and a bundle of dried moss. Striking the flints together, he shot sparks into the moss until it began to smoulder, and then very carefully added fragments of stick, blowing all the while to encourage the tiny flame. Slowly, the flame grew stronger and brighter, lighting up a circle barely wider than his hand to begin with, and finally swelling out to illuminate the whole cave.

What he saw in that flickering light appalled him. Strewn all over the floor were the remnants of savage meals: bones and skulls and twisted broken shapes, many with the skin and putrid flesh still hanging from them. Great gouts of frozen blood stuck to the walls and ceiling, and piles of mangled entrails, torn from the unlucky victims, had been gathered into grisly heaps. Tal could see at a glance that most of the creatures had not been eaten: they had been brought there merely to satisfy Shadroth's lust for destruction. From a score of sightless skulls, unseeing eyes stared at him in the dim uncertain light, as though pleading for a mercy which they had not received.

The sight of all that pointless carnage aroused in Tal a confused feeling of pity and disgust. Here, before him, was the grim proof of all that Shadroth represented. A futile act of cruelty, the killing of the Feln, had first awakened him; and now it was the same kind of cruelty which sustained him. He was in truth the incarnation of that violence which killed without reason or purpose; which destroyed others not for food, but for the sheer pleasure of the hunt.

Almost overcome with nausea once again, Tal leaned against the side wall with his eyes closed. During that minute or two of silence and inaction, all fear left him. In its place, he experienced a surge of rage at what he had discovered. From the near-by opening, he heard the Feln's snarl of anger, a sound which seemed to echo his own deep sense of outrage; and when he opened his eyes he was inspired by a new spirit of determination. Secretly, he swore to himself that, come what may, Shadroth would be defeated, even if it meant hunting him down as Ubek had suggested.

Perhaps it was that new spirit of determination which cleared his vision, for he now looked past the torn and mutilated flesh to what he had been searching for all along. In the far corner of the cave, next to a wide passage which burrowed back into the hillside, was what surely had to be Shadroth's nest, the place where he waited out the hours of daylight. It was made from the blackened bones of innumerable victims. Hundreds of them had been pushed together into a great heap which had then been hollowed out in the centre to form a roughly circular cavity – a fitting nesting place for anything as hateful as Shadroth.

All his earlier nervousness gone, Tal picked his way carefully between the limbs and bodies which littered the floor of the cave and climbed up onto the rim of the nest. The smell here was worse than ever, but he endured it as best he could – one hand held over his nose and mouth, while with the other he pulled aside what remained of the carcass of an antelope. He hoped to find a large fragment of claw and for several minutes he hunted feverishly amongst the bones – but without success. All that he uncovered were thick black hairs which had fallen from Shadroth's coat.

Disappointed, he climbed down from the nest and went back to the far side of the cave, where he added sticks to the fire. What good were those hairs to him, he thought bitterly, as he crouched before the flames. He needed something more practical, something he could hunt and fight with. A sharp tooth, for instance, that could be put into his sling and . . .

He stood up suddenly, a smile spreading slowly across his face. Yes, that was what he needed after all. Not some hard projectile, like a claw or tooth, to be shot from a sling; but the sling itself – the long black hairs plaited together to form the strings, the same hairs woven into a tight circle that could serve as a cup to hold the stones. Not ordinary stones either: more of the hairs wound tightly around sharp flints. A weapon truly fit to face Shadroth with; fashioned completely from his night-black coat.

As Tal's confidence increased, a plan quickly formed itself in his mind. Clearly, the thing for him to do was to make the sling there and then; and afterwards to lie in wait below the causeway. If he attacked Shadroth in the early dawn, he, Tal, would have the advantage. Also, if his strategy failed, he would have a good chance of escaping: Shadroth would be unwilling to pursue him in the growing daylight.

But the night was already far advanced and he had no time to lose. Hurrying across the cave, he climbed back into the nest and began gathering the longest and thickest of the hairs. He hardly noticed the disgusting smell now; nor did he so much as glance at his tomb-like surroundings. All his attention was given to the making of the long plaited strings with which he hoped to destroy Shadroth. The hairs proved to be tough and pliable, like pieces of soft wire, not particularly easy to plait. But he persevered, pausing only to heap more wood on the fire.

In the light of the leaping flames, he completed the strings and the circular cup and tied them deftly together. Once, twice, he whirled the sling around his head to check its weight and feel. It was heavier than he was used to, but otherwise strong and perfectly balanced. There remained now only the stones to be bound: and selecting seven of the sharpest flints from his pouch, he began to wrap each of them in a length of hair.

That final task proved more difficult than he had expected – the binding kept coming loose or slipping off altogether – and he was still struggling with it when a faint whispering began outside. It was a familiar enough sound: the murmur of lightly falling rain. Perhaps that's why he didn't really notice it. The Feln, after all, was on guard; and while she remained silent, there was nothing for him to fear.

With a sigh of satisfaction, he secured the hair-binding on the last stone and stood up. For the first time he became consciously aware of the rain, which had now been falling for some time. His initial reaction was to feel glad: since Shadroth's coming, there had been little enough rain and the Greenlands were beginning to look dryer than he had ever seen them. The much-needed moisture would revive the sagging vines and freshen the drooping foliage.

But all at once another consideration occurred to Tal. Shadroth hated and feared the river because it was the source of all life in the Greenlands. Would he perhaps respond in the same way to the rain? Was he at that very moment hurrying back to the safety and shelter of his lair? It was a distinct possibility, and with a sinking sense of having lingered too long, Tal quickly left the cave.

The Feln, as faithful as ever, was still waiting outside. She seemed relieved not only to see him again, but also to leave that dreadful place. There was in her deep yellow eyes a gleam of warning, as though she realized that time was running out for them. Flicking her tail from side to side, she edged away from the cave mouth, obviously impatient to get away; and at a signal from Tal, she turned and loped off into the driving rain.

As far as Tal could remember, there was only one place where they could leave the causeway: that was down the steep zigzag path they had climbed earlier. Whatever else happened, they had to reach that path before Shadroth. It was their one line of retreat; if it were cut off, they would be trapped up there in the open. With this thought to spur him on, Tal ran as fast as he could along the winding slope.

Before they had covered more than half the distance, however, the Feln suddenly slithered to a halt, pulling up so abruptly that Tal almost crashed into her. It was not difficult to guess what had made her stop: the hair along the back of her neck was standing straight up and her fangs were bared in a silent snarl. Crouching close beside her, Tal peered apprehensively into the darkness. For a while, nothing happened: the only movement was a slight stirring of the breeze; the only sound, the whisper of the falling rain. A flicker of hope started inside him – and was immediately extinguished as the Feln let out a soft growl and, almost simultaneously, the wound in his forehead gave an initial warning throb.

He didn't wait for any clearer sign. Leaping to his feet, and with the Feln close behind, he sprinted back up the way they had just come. There was, as he admitted afterwards, nothing reasonable about that flight: it was merely a reflex action, an unthinking response to the evil which was steadily advancing up the causeway. Not until the black mouth of the cave again loomed up before them did he fully realize how foolish they had been. Had they continued down the slope, there was the faint chance that they might have reached the path before Shadroth. Now, they were trapped in a cul-de-sac.

The Feln, balked by the cave, ran frantically to the edge of the causeway and leaned over. For an instant, Tal feared that she was going to jump – with the hillside several hundred feet below them, she couldn't possibly have survived.

'No!' he cried out frantically.

That urgent warning seemed to steady both of them: the Feln drew back and moved calmly to his side; and Tal, recapturing some of his former determination, slipped the dull black sling from his belt and loaded it with one of the specially prepared stones.

Yet, unfortunately, what had steadied them had served as a warning to Shadroth. From far down the causeway, through the rain and darkness, came the high chilling wail of his death cry – and with it, the throbbing pain in Tal's forehead intensified. As Shadroth rapidly drew nearer, the pain increased, and Tal had to concentrate with all his might to keep his vision clear. He knew that he would not have very much time in which to act and he began whirling the sling slowly around his head, waiting for the first gleam from those glowing red eyes. But as always, it was the rush of icy cold which came first, like a blast of wind from a land of eternal winter. Tal felt the Feln stiffen and tremble beside him, the fur on her sides, already tipped with frost, rubbing against his leg. He heard her growl and choke as she fought for breath, but still she held her ground. They had not long to wait now, he was sure of that.

'Come on,' he muttered to himself, 'show yourself.'

The sling was whirling fast above his head; all his muscles were tensed in readiness. Fighting off the dulling pain which pressed like a great weight upon his skull, he probed the rain-filled night for a glimpse of the enemy. He thought that he would at least get some warning – a dim outline; a flash from those red eyes. Yet he was completely unprepared for what happened next. It was as if every vestige of light had suddenly disappeared from the world, the darkness closing in on them from every side. All around them the rain, frozen even before it could hit the ground, fell in tiny splinters of ice. And there, high above them, filling the whole width of the causeway, was

138

Shadroth. He was like the night itself, only his small malicious eyes, glowing fiercely, betraying his presence. Again the death cry rang out, so close that it almost deafened them: and at that very instant, Tal released the stone.

He didn't hear it hit, but he knew it had found its mark by the way Shadroth's scream of triumph changed abruptly to a shriek of agony. That cry carried the same note of pain and anguish that Tal had heard down there in the Greenlands, when he had struck the black charm. Momentarily, the causeway trembled beneath their feet; and as it did so, Shadroth's impenetrable darkness seemed to vibrate and dissolve, the hate-filled eyes to blink and go out. As the huge shadow screeched and fell back, the fire inside the cave flickered into life, casting a pale light onto the strip of stony ground on which Tal and the Feln stood. For the space of a breath or two, Tal actually believed that he had won: that the Greenlands were free at last; that the broken bodies which littered the cave behind him were avenged.

But his hope was short-lived. Hardly had he reloaded the sling than Shadroth's probing, demented eyes were once more hovering above them, his icy breath cutting through the darkness like an invisible knife. Again Tal released one of the hair-wound stones; and again Shadroth screamed in agony and drew back. It was clear now, though, that he was by no means defeated. The sling, while it could keep him at bay, lacked the power to destroy him. And soon he was advancing as determinedly as before.

Twice more Tal fired stones from the sling – each time with the same effect. Still Shadroth rallied and bore down on them once again. If they stood their ground, Tal realized grimly, there could be only one outcome. Already the Feln was incapable of defending herself: hunched beside him, she was coughing and choking, struggling for breath.

For the fifth time he reloaded the sling. His movements were unhurried and deliberate. He knew now what had to be done, and with only two other stones left in his pouch there was little room for error. Dropping down onto one knee in order to steady himself further, he waited until Shadroth was almost upon them. Then, instead of aiming the stone into the mass of advancing blackness, he shot it straight at the hateful gleaming eyes.

The effect was just what he had hoped for. Shadroth didn't merely retreat a short distance. His great shadowy bulk appeared to twist and gyrate, almost to shrivel under the impact of that telling blow. With a high-pitched screech which stirred the boulders on the surrounding hills, he staggered away from the cave, withdrawing to a position of safety, his glowing eyes fading back into the night.

That brief pause gave Tal exactly the opportunity he needed. Grasping the Feln by the neck, he coaxed and tugged her round until she faced the cave. Her fur was covered in a glistening sheet of frost, and she was so cold that she found it difficult to move. But she understood what was expected of her; and overcoming her natural repugnance, she followed him into the cave on stiff, shaking legs.

Tal, still unaffected by the freezing temperature, went quickly over to the fire and plucked from it one of the burning logs. At the far end of the cave, beside the ghastly nest of bones, was the opening of the passage or tunnel that he had noticed earlier. He had no idea where it led – or, indeed, whether it led anywhere at all. But the insistent pain in his forehead warned him that Shadroth had recovered from that last blow and was already advancing up the causeway. There was only one option open to them now. And with the Feln close on his heels, he picked his way through the decaying bodies of Shadroth's victims and stepped into the jagged mouth of the tunnel.

17. The Cavern

The Feln, suffering badly from the unnatural cold, could do little more than hobble feebly after Tal. In that condition she was no match for the speed and power of Shadroth. What saved her from immediate death was the fire in the cave. The light, flickering on the walls of his lair, made Shadroth pause suspiciously and hesitate several minutes before entering. By then, Tal and the Feln were well along the tunnel, at a point where it forked in two different directions. One passage, wide and inviting, spiralled upwards; the other, narrow and forbidding, sloped down further into the hillside. The choice facing Tal was a difficult one: with all his heart, he longed to get out of these tunnels, up into the freedom of the open air. On the other hand, the immediate task was to escape from Shadroth, and that meant going where he could not follow.

Standing there, torn by indecision, he heard Shadroth scream with rage as he entered the cave and stamped out the remains of the fire. That insane cry, echoing ominously along the tunnel towards him, helped Tal to decide. And with the burning log held out before him, he crouched low and entered the narrower of the two openings.

Within a dozen paces, the tunnel had narrowed even further, the roof so low that Tal was forced down onto his hands and knees. In such a confined space, both he and the Feln were reasonably secure from Shadroth. But now a new terror presented itself: what if this tunnel led nowhere? What if it narrowed down to nothing, ending in a wall of rock? Tal noticed with alarm that already the air was becoming stale and unwholesome; the log that he carried, their only source of light, was burning low. Had they escaped from Shadroth only to perish here, in this tomb of dry stone?

Such thoughts filled him with dismay. Yet in spite of his gnawing anxiety, he continued to crawl on: whatever lay ahead could be no worse than what they had left behind them. That was one small consolation. The other was the fact that the Feln was still following him. Surely, Tal reasoned with himself, she would not go on unless there was some point in doing so. Behind him, he could hear her heavy breathing and the even shuffle of her great paws as she forced her way along in the confined space. The continual movement had warmed her, brought back some of her natural suppleness, and despite her size she was finding the difficult conditions easier to cope with than Tal. Time and again, she bumped gently against him, as though urging him to hurry.

Tal needed very little urging, for yet another problem had arisen: the log which he held out before him was beginning to burn low. It was bad enough squirming along the narrow tunnel with a light to guide him: in the darkness it would be nothing short of a nightmare. Yet there was no avoiding that nightmare. Several times he stopped and blew on the coals, trying to coax them into life. But all his care could not prevent the flame from burning lower and lower, until soon there was only a small red glow showing between ridges of black charcoal. And finally that too faded to nothing.

The first few moments of total darkness terrified him. He froze exactly where he was, unable to move, feeling that he could hardly breathe. The Feln growled gently and nudged at him; but it made no difference. He was sure that this was the end; there was no point in going any further. With that certainty, something seemed to give way inside him. It was just as though he had been hanging on the edge of a cliff for a long time, with no real hope of climbing to safety: now, at last, he could let go. And there, in the silence and darkness, with no other human being to observe him, he gave himself up to the bitter tears of despair.

The Feln didn't move or make a sound while he cried. He forgot she was even there, so taken up was he with his own grief. He imagined that he was entirely alone; deserted by everybody; left there to die a horrible and futile death. As his tears gradually subsided, he felt the awful stillness of the rocky hillside press down on him, burying him alive. He no longer had the will to struggle against it; he almost welcomed the deadening effect of the unbroken silence. He closed his eyes and let his cheek fall onto the hard rock, ready to give in completely – and at that very moment felt something warm and moist on his leg.

It was the Feln, licking him gently and reassuringly in the darkness, much as she might have licked a young Feln cub had it been frightened and uncertain. Never, since his earliest childhood when he had been nursed by his grandfather, had Tal been so grateful for the warm contact of another living creature. The soft, slightly rasping touch of her tongue on his bare skin seemed to lift the weight of darkness from him and to banish his despair. He thought again of Lea, truly alone in the Greenlands, without the comfort and the companionship of the Feln to help her; and with a renewed sense of purpose, he wiped the tears from his cheeks and began to inch his way along the tunnel once more.

It was no easy task without a light to guide him. Every few yards he would bang his head or scrape his elbow or shoulder against outjutting pieces of rock; and more than once, when he stopped to rest, the sweat streaming from his limbs, he seriously wondered whether he possessed the determination to go on. But always the Feln was there behind him, nudging him encouragingly, the soft purr of her breath reminding him of the life and freedom which awaited him in the world above.

Perhaps the worst thing of all was his ignorance of whether the tunnel was sloping up or down. It was impossible to tell in the darkness. Surrounded on every side by a black wall of night, he had lost any clear sense of space. All he could do was continue crawling on in the faint hope that the tunnel would somehow lead them to safety.

After nearly two hours the crawling motion became almost natural to him. With fixed mechanical movements, he pressed forward, no longer bothering to check the width of the tunnel or the height of the roof above his head. The first inkling he had that his surroundings had changed was when he sensed something moving to his left. Reaching out, he found that the Feln was standing beside him. Without his realizing it, the tunnel had widened. Carefully, hardly daring to hope, he reached up: the roof was already sufficiently high for him to crouch. Within a few paces, he was able to stand upright. And only a short distance further on, he was overjoyed to feel a breath of fresh morning air brush his cheek.

With arms stretched out before him, he hurried towards the source of that fresh air – blundering into unseen walls, tripping over loose boulders. But he hardly noticed the knocks and bruises now; not with freedom so close. After each fall, he picked himself up and groped his way on. Already he was able to make out the dim outline of floor and ceiling as the darkness became tinged with grey. That meant the dawn had come. Eagerly he broke into a stumbling run – and suddenly stopped, blinded by a circle of daylight which appeared directly ahead of him.

After so long in the total obscurity of the tunnel, he could not endure the bright sunlight, and he turned away and buried his face in his hands. He stayed like that for some time, letting only a little of the light seep between his fingers, slowly accustoming his eyes to the painful brightness. Only when he could see clearly and without discomfort did he lower his hands and look around.

He found that he was in a large airy cavern – larger even than Shadroth's lair – with a single wide-mouthed entrance that looked out across the sunlit hillside. It appeared to be uninhabited and was completely bare except for a tall slab of rock which stood upright in the middle of the floor and reached up to the roof. Tal had never entered the cavern before – he was sure of that. And yet there was definitely something familiar about it.

He needed only a moment or two to realize why that should be so: this was the place he had seen in the vision, when the Gift had possessed him; the place where a giant version of himself was destined to face Shadroth. Yes, the single curve of the walls and roof was the same, a great arch of solid rock;

there were the holes in the floor where the flares would be burning, lighting the fearful contest; and over there ... He frowned, mystified by what he saw. In the exact place where his own gigantic likeness would stand was the upright slab of rock. Puzzled, he walked over to inspect it. It was smooth, unblemished, solid, probably weighing many tons, and was pinned firmly between the floor and roof. It would have been extremely difficult to move. Even that larger-than-life figure in his vision would have been hard-pressed to displace it – and why should that figure wish to do so anyway?

With a sigh, he gave up trying to understand the strange contradiction of his vision and left the cavern. But outside, another surprise awaited him. The cavern itself, which he had assumed to be a natural hollow in the hillside, was not really that at all. Above him towered an almost vertical cliff. At some time in the past, a whole section of the cliff had broken away and fallen. It was the fallen section that now formed the cavern. What prevented it collapsing under its own enormous weignt or sliding down the hillside was the single upright slab of rock that stood inside. Like a pillar, that rock supported the whole structure.

More mystified than ever, Tal turned away and followed the Feln down the hillside. After the overnight rain, the Greenlands were sparkling and green below him, and the air was fresh and cool. Warmed by the early morning sun, he breathed deeply, glad simply to be alive and well. Although he was physically tired, he was otherwise unaffected by his recent ordeal. Already, there in the light and air, the happenings of the night seemed far behind him. The only visible reminder of all that he had been through was the jet-black sling that swung from his belt.

Like the Feln, he was hungry and thirsty as well as tired. But he knew there was something more important than his own comfort, and that was Lea's safety. Before he did anything else, he had to make sure she wasn't lying dead or injured somewhere near the river.

That image, of Lea frozen or struck down by Shadroth, cast a kind of veil over the natural brightness of the day, and Tal consciously quickened his pace. What worried him more than anything else was the thought that she might be injured and in pain, unable to move or signal for help. That thought didn't bother him for long, though. He had not been walking for more than half an hour when he heard his own name being called, and there, far over on his right, was Lea hurrying towards him.

A few minutes later, breathless but happy, they were standing with their arms around each other.

'You're safe!' Tal cried, astonished and relieved at the same time.

'And you?' Lea asked, an edge of concern to her voice.

She ran her hands gently over Tal's arms and shoulders, where the skin had been scarred and grazed by the difficult journey through the tunnel.

'Oh, that's not serious,' Tal said. 'Far more important is what happened to you last night.'

'That's easily told,' Lea said. 'Nothing happened.'

'Nothing?'

'Nothing at all. I don't mind admitting, I was terrified once the sun went down. I expected Shadroth to appear at any moment, but he never came near me. In the end, I just stopped where I was, a short distance from the river, and waited. It was so peaceful in the Greenlands that I actually dozed off a few times. What woke me up, two or three hours before dawn, was hearing Shadroth scream out from somewhere near his lair. I thought perhaps he was attacking you and I set out straight away. That's how I got here so soon.'

'Yes, he was attacking us,' Tal said, 'up there on the causeway.'

And briefly, he recounted the events of the previous night, including his discovery of the strange cave which he had seen once before in a vision. When he had finished, Lea shook her head in bewilderment.

'The main point is that you're still alive,' she said. 'That's more important than anything else. Still, I wish there weren't so many things that continue to puzzle me about Shadroth. For instance, where was he for most of last night? He wasn't following me; and he returned to his lair only in the early hours of the morning.'

'He could have been visiting the Slopes,' Tal suggested.

'Yes,' Lea agreed, 'but why? What's the point? Surely we're the main threat to him now. It's true we can't destroy him. But in the past few days we've managed to hurt him twice. Why isn't he doing everything in his power to track us down and kill us?'

Tal shrugged.

'I don't understand it either,' he said.

'And that's not the only thing,' Lea went on. 'There's this business about the cave you've just discovered. Why should you choose to face Shadroth there? And how can you ever grow to such a size or replace that great rock you told me about? None of it makes sense to me.'

'Nor to me,' Tal said. 'Yet it must mean something. The Gift is never wrong. The things it shows you always come true in the end.'

'But how can *this* vision come true?' Lea said doubtfully. 'You can't suddenly grow to giant size. Nobody can. And even if you could, why would you be holding up the roof of that cave?'

She turned impatiently away and stared down at where the Feln was waiting for them. While they'd been talking, the huge cat had been pacing restlessly to and fro, as though unwilling to remain there on the bare hillside.

'Is something the matter with her?' Lea asked.

'I think she's thirsty,' Tal said. 'I know I am. It was hot dry work crawling along that tunnel, and we haven't had a drink since yesterday evening.'

'Oh, that's easily fixed,' Lea said. 'There's a hollow over there, where last night's rain has gathered.'

She pointed back across the hillside and, without waiting for a reply, set off. As they walked, she chattered on about the previous evening; but Tal, wearing a thoughtful expression, was only half listening. Something Lea had said a little earlier had intrigued him. It was the part about his holding up the roof of the cave. He had not thought of the vision in quite that way: he had only considered the question of how he could possibly replace the slab of rock. But of course she was right: if, somehow, he did manage to replace it, then he would have to support the roof. Without that support, the whole cave would come crashing down.

He was still pondering this question when they came over a rise and saw a clear pool in the hollow below them. The Feln, scenting the water, broke into a run and reached it long before they did. Just when she was about to drink, however, something odd occurred. As she leaned forward, she caught a glimpse of her own reflection staring up at her and, momentarily startled, she leaped back. Whether she was nervous after their adventures in the tunnel, or whether it was the absolute stillness of the pool which misled her, Tal was never sure. Certainly she recovered from her surprise almost immediately and was soon lapping contentedly at the water. But that brief error had already had its effect on Tal who, in a sudden flash of insight, had understood the meaning of his own vision.

'Yes, that's the answer!' he burst out.

Lea paused and looked back.

'What is the answer?' she asked.

'You must have noticed what happened to the Feln just now,' he said excitedly. 'She thought the face in the pool was real! She didn't realize it was only a reflection!'

'Yes, I did notice,' Lea answered. 'Why is that so important?'

'Because that's how we'll trick Shadroth!' Tal almost shouted. 'That giant image of myself, the one I saw in the vision, well it isn't real at all. And it doesn't replace the supporting rock. It's just a large painting!'

'A painting?' Lea asked.

'Yes. We'll paint my likeness on the smooth slab of rock. It will only look like me. At night, in the dim light of the torches, Shadroth won't be able to tell the difference.'

'You really think we can trick Shadroth like that?' Lea said uncertainly.

'I'm sure of it,' Tal said, laughing now with relief, 'especially if we can make him angry beforehand. If we can get him into a rage, he won't have time to think: he'll just rush at whatever looks like the enemy – he'll attack the rock itself. And then . . .'

He left the rest unspoken as a light of understanding spread slowly across Lea's face.

'So that's what Molani meant,' she murmured.

Tal nodded.

'We made a mistake last night,' he replied, 'but we won't make the same mistake again. It's just as Molani said: Shadroth can be destroyed only by himself. He alone possesses the necessary power.'

18. The Conflict

The days that followed were busy ones for both of them. Fired with a new sense of purpose, they rose before dawn and worked through until dusk, not even stopping in the heat of the day. Their first task was to collect the colours they would need for the painting. In this Tal was expert. He knew which leaves to gather and boil down in order to make reds and blues, and which rocks to crush for yellows and browns. He also searched for a certain root, which, when pounded with a stone, splayed out to form a stiff, fibrous brush. Meanwhile, Lea dug for the blue-grey clay that lay beneath the soft surface soil of the Greenlands. This she moulded carefully into round pots that she dried in the sun and then baked in a hot fire. It was in these pots that they mixed and blended the colours Tal would use.

Throughout this period of activity, they took shelter at night in the narrow-mouthed cave that they had located on their journey back from the Grasslands. There, they were safe from both Shadroth and members of the Clan; and also close to the large cavern in which the painting had to be done. The first night in this new refuge was a nervous one. After Tal's visit to the lair, they expected Shadroth to seek them out. But as before he hardly came near them. Once or twice, soon after dark, Tal detected his presence outside, but he lingered there only a few minutes before moving off.

They were thankful for Shadroth's absence, because it left them free to carry out their plan, but also slightly concerned by it.

'Shadroth can't think we're much of a threat to him,' Lea said one evening, when they were sitting together in the safety of the cave. 'If he did, he wouldn't ignore us like this.'

It was exactly the thought which had been worrying Tal for some time and he had no convincing answer ready.

'Perhaps there's a greater threat to him elsewhere,' he replied.

It seemed the only possible explanation, and yet neither he nor Lea really believed in it.

Fortunately for them, they were so busy that they had little time to sit and worry. The painting itself had now been started and it demanded all Tal's skill and attention. He had never attempted anything on such a large scale before and to begin with he worked slowly and hesitantly, unsure of his own abilities. Had he not possessed the Gift, it is doubtful whether he would ever have completed it. As it was, he was unhappy with his own work: it failed to match the vivid picture in his mind; it was too flat, too static; and each evening, when he hurried away through the waning light, he felt depressed by the little he had achieved. Even when the figure was almost complete, he continued to be disappointed by it. Always there was something wrong: the face; the drawing of the hands; the positioning of the legs. Perched on a dry log which they had dragged into the cave, he would repaint portions of the figure over and over again – and afterwards feel just as dissatisfied. Nothing he could do would really bring the figure to life; always, in spite of his efforts, it remained flat and uninteresting.

Eventually, it was Lea who persuaded him to stop.

'There's no use in going on,' she said. 'It's as good as it's ever going to be. The time has come to put it to the test.'

Tired and dispirited after his day's work, Tal gave in without an argument, and it was agreed that they should make the final preparations on the following day.

Up until then they had seen very little of the Feln: while Tal had been painting, she had spent most of her time away from them, down in the Greenlands. But now, with her usual uncanny ability to know when she was needed most, she returned. They were sitting in the sun making flares from dried rushes when she came trotting up the slope and lay down between them. Lea looked across at Tal and smiled.

'At least someone believes in what we're doing,' she said.

Tal reached out and stroked the fine golden head.

'It's a good sign, her coming back to us now,' he replied.

Although they still dreaded what lay ahead, they felt distinctly heartened by the Feln's reappearance, and for the rest of the day they applied themselves more cheerfully to the few remaining tasks. By late afternoon, all was ready: the flares were in position and a small fire was burning just inside the cave entrance. Their plan was a very simple one: Lea would remain behind, ready to light the flares; and Tal would try to lure Shadroth back to the cave.

Shortly before dusk, he and the Feln set off. As usual, she appeared calm and relaxed, moving easily across the rocky slope. By contrast, Tal felt tense and anxious, and kept nervously fingering the black sling which hung from his belt. The very thought of what soon had to be done made him break out in a sweat; and at the bottom of the steep path which led up to the causeway, he paused for a few minutes, breathing deeply, until he had calmed down. Only when the frantic hammering of his heart had quietened did he begin the ascent. But that brief delay was vital. Before he could reach the top, a rush of cold air swept past them as Shadroth hurried down towards the rapidly darkening Greenlands.

Angry with himself for having missed his chance, he returned, shamefaced, to the cave.

'Never mind,' Lea said soothingly, 'we can try again at dawn. At least if anything goes wrong we'll have the daylight to protect us.'

For the remainder of that night they tried to sleep, but without success. The knowledge of what still awaited them kept them restless and watchful, and the last few hours were spent huddled together beside the fire talking quietly. It was the Feln who roused them to action once more. Sensing that the dawn was not far off, she went over to the cave mouth and looked back inquiringly at Tal. Determined not to fail again, he rose instantly to his feet and, with whispered encouragement from Lea, stole quietly outside.

At that time in the morning the moon was low in the sky, and Tal was glad of the Feln to guide him over the rock-strewn ground. They made good time to the bottom of the path and climbed quickly up to the edge of the causeway. From there, they could see the Greenlands, like a sea of shadow, stretching away below them. Not a breath of wind stirred; and although Tal strained to listen, he could not hear so much as the cry of a bird. All was still and quiet, as though sunk in sleep.

Carefully, he removed the deadly sling from his belt and loaded it with one of the two remaining stones that were wound with hair. After that there was nothing to do but wait. Knowing how well Shadroth's glowing eyes could see in the dark, he stayed out of sight, below the edge of the causeway, watching the eastern sky for the first sign of breaking day. Gradually the dark curve of the sky changed to grey and then to a murky whiteness. Below them, the Greenlands were still immersed in night; but up there on the open hillside the darkness was slowly beginning to disperse. Tal wondered fleetingly whether Shadroth had already returned and was sheltering securely in his lair. But hardly had that thought passed through his mind than the throbbing pain in his forehead told him otherwise.

The Feln, reminded suddenly of her earlier experience, snarled and backed away down the path. Tal would have liked nothing better than to follow her, but he knew there must be no mistake now. Standing up, he peered cautiously over the edge of the causeway. Sunrise was still some time away and it was too dark to see clearly. Nonetheless, there was just enough grey light in the sky to reveal the murky outline of dense black shadow that was moving up towards him from the Greenlands. It was gliding across the uneven ground with astonishing speed, far faster than a man or even one of the Feln could run, and in a very short time had gained the bottom of the causeway. As it approached, growing larger and more forbidding with every passing second, Tal stepped back a pace or two and steadied himself on the steeply sloping ground. Then, ignoring the sharp pain in his head, he began whirling the sling.

He had no intention of allowing Shadroth to approach too closely this time. With the sling turning at top speed, he hurled the stone with all his might as soon as Shadroth came within range. Nor did he wait to see if his aim was true. While the stone was still speeding towards its mark, he turned and bounded down the steep track. Far behind him, the long piercing scream told him that the stone had found its target. But still he didn't stop. He was at the bottom of the path now and running for all he was worth through the melting darkness. Once, missing his footing on the rough surface, he fell headlong; but he was up in an instant, running harder than ever.

Somewhere in the background, he heard rocks crashing from the causeway as Shadroth, recovering from the impact of the stone, followed them down the narrow path. It was exactly what Tal had intended; yet he was also horrified at the thought of that vast black body bearing down upon him. Pushing himself to the very limits of his strength, he leaped and scrambled over the broken jumble of rocks which lay in his way. Whatever else happened, he had to keep far enough ahead; at all costs, he had to reach the cave before Shadroth.

Yet despite his fierce determination, the massive shadow which was pursuing them drew ever closer. A gust of freezing air swept past Tal, chilling the ground beneath his feet. The Feln, responding instinctively to that icy touch, increased her pace. But try as he might, Tal could go no faster. Again the cold wind blew past him, transforming the morning dew into tiny crystals of ice that glimmered in the growing light. Without slowing down, Tal groped in his leather pouch for the last of the hair-wound stones. The cave was not far ahead of him now and he knew this final blow must be a telling one. Resisting the desire to dodge aside or defend himself, he ran straight on until he was completely enveloped in a cloud of freezing air. Only then did he turn, the sling already whirling in his hand.

Above him reared the dense blackness that was Shadroth, the two eyes gleaming at him with evil intent. At such close range he couldn't possibly miss: the stone streaked from the sling, straight into the vast hollow space between the eyes. He heard it strike, biting into the coarse protective hair, and Shadroth screamed horribly and fell back, the darkness wavering for a moment, threatening to merge back into the waning shadows of night. It was the chance Tal needed. Before Shadroth could recover, he had scrambled the last hundred paces up the slope and run gasping for breath into the mouth of the cave.

What he found there came as such a surprise that he was stopped in his tracks. Just inside the entrance was a half-circle of burning flares; and beyond them, a gigantic living image of himself. It no longer looked at all like the painting that had so disappointed him. In the smoky atmosphere the supporting rock was almost invisible; it merged with the black background, giving the impression that the painted figure was standing free and unsupported. The uncertain colouring, which had shown up badly by day, now appeared entirely lifelike; and the once stiff, ungainly limbs, caught in the shifting light of the flares, seemed to stir and move, as though they were filled with life.

The transformation was so complete that even Tal was taken aback. He felt that he was actually facing a larger, fiercer version of himself; and he stood there for several precious seconds before he gathered his wits and ran through the half-circle of flares and past the rock to where Lea and the Feln were waiting for him in the narrow passage.

He had no sooner crouched beside them than a shadow fell across the main entrance of the cave, blotting out the grey morning sky. Moments later, Shadroth himself appeared: huge, shaggy-coated, he squeezed his great bulk through the opening and stood up. Never had he looked more massive and terrifying. Undeterred by the light from the flares, his tiny eyes glinting blood-red, he gazed balefully at the enemy who had eluded him for so long. He showed no hesitation, no uncertainty about the giant figure which now confronted him. Consumed by his desire for revenge, half-blinded by his frustrated anger and hatred, he was completely misled by the painting. All he could see through the mist of his own rage was the likeness of the boy who bore his mark. With a roar, he beat the ground so hard that the hillside trembled. Then, moving with incredible speed, he lunged forward and struck the supporting rock a single punishing blow which broke it in two.

What happened next was difficult to follow in the noise and confusion. Shadroth, encountering rock rather than the living flesh he expected, cried out in pain and alarm. And simultaneously, the overarching cave, no longer supported by the central pillar, cracked in two and came crashing down onto the hillside.

Neither Tal nor Lea actually saw the cave collapse. In the company of the Feln, they had scurried further into the narrow tunnel and thrown themselves face down on the ground, their arms held protectively over their heads. They remained like that until the crashing and rumbling had stopped – and only then crept back to witness the devastation.

The cave itself had ceased to exist. At the entrance to the tunnel, they found themselves standing in the light of early dawn. Before them, where the cave had once been, was a great pile of shattered stone over which the settling dust hovered like smoke. As they watched, the sun rose above the distant cliffs, bathing the whole dismal scene in a gentle yellow wash of light and warmth.

'We've done it!' Tal said in a whisper. 'We've destroyed him!'

'Do you think he's under all that?' Lea asked, far less certain than Tal.

'He's been crushed,' Tal said triumphantly, 'destroyed by his own strength, the way Molani predicted.'

The Feln, meanwhile, had picked her way across the rubble to approximately the spot where the pillar had stood. Her uneasy growl drew their attention and they clambered over towards her. There, at her feet, splashed across a shard of rock, was a glistening, jet-black streak of Shadroth's blood. The stench of it, like the smell of rotting flesh in the lair, made Tal gag, and he turned away. Behind him, he heard Lea say:

'You must be right: he's probably buried beneath our feet.'

But Tal had already seen something which dashed his earlier hopes.

'Look!' he said.

He pointed beyond the rubble to a similar glistening streak of blood and, further away still, to another patch of it. With their eyes, they followed the bloody trail across the hillside to the bottom of the zigzag path and then up towards the causeway. They were just in time to see a blur of black shadow vanish into the waiting mouth of the lair.

'Can nothing destroy him?' Tal murmured, unable to keep the disappointment out of his voice. He turned towards Lea, feeling suddenly shaken by all that had happened. 'What else can we do after this?' he asked.

She was gazing at the distant lair, her mouth set in a grim line.

'Whatever else we do,' she said warningly, 'we must leave here. It won't be safe any longer in that tiny cave. He'll be determined to destroy us now that we've succeeded in injuring him. And we've seen what he can do even to hard rock. The only secure place will be the cave behind the falls.'

She clambered across the jagged tumble of rocks towards the open hillside, the Feln beside her. But when she glanced back, Tal had vanished.

'Tal!' she called out urgently.

His voice, strangely muffled, came from somewhere beneath the jumble of rocks.

'I'm here,' he called back, 'wait a minute.'

She waited, listening to him scrabbling in amongst the rubble. When at last he reappeared, he was holding several strands of Shadroth's wiry hair and no fewer than five thick black claws, each of them longer than a hunting knife. They were razor sharp and all but one of them ended in a deadly point.

'What do you want those for?' Lea asked fearfully.

'I'll show you,' Tal said.

He knelt down in the dust and laid the claws out in the shape of a star. At the centre of the star, the thick ends of the claws criss-crossed slightly, and these he bound together with wiry strands of hair. When he had finished, he had a star-knife made completely from the night-black body of Shadroth.

Lea had been watching him with some concern.

'Aren't you coming with me to the falls?' she asked.

He stood up.

'Yes, I'm coming,' he said, 'but we're not running away any longer. When Shadroth seeks us out, we'll be ready for him.'

And he held the dull black star menacingly above his head, its shadow masking his eyes in a way that made Lea shiver.

19. Dilemma

They reached the falls shortly after midday and spent the rest of the afternoon gathering fresh fruit from the trees and bushes which grew near the river. Walking alone along the pathways, Tal could not escape a feeling of uneasiness. There was a brooding quality about the Greenlands, an air of restless uncertainty. At his approach, the tiny squirrel-tailed apes screeched in alarm and went swinging away through the tree-tops. Even the birds sounded warning notes as he drew near. Yet he sensed that it wasn't just his presence, nor the dull black star-knife hanging from his belt, that inspired such widespread concern. There was an atmosphere of fear, almost of threat, hanging over everything, tingeing with darkness the speckled sunlight through which he walked.

The tension within the Greenlands seemed only to increase as the afternoon wore on. When he met Lea back at the falls, she too was troubled by it.

'It's like waiting for a great storm to break,' she said, trying to smile at him. 'Thank goodness we have the cave to shelter in.'

But Tal shook his head.

'We can't achieve anything by cowering in there,' he said. 'We've managed to injure Shadroth. What we must do now is make sure he doesn't have time to recover.'

'You mean actually go out against him?' Lea asked.

'Yes, we wouldn't have to go far. We could lie in wait for him just a short distance from the river. He'd never expect that. And we do have the star-knife to protect us.'

'To protect us, or to attack Shadroth with?' she asked.

Tal shrugged.

'Perhaps both,' he said vaguely.

At that moment, with the afternoon rapidly drawing to a close, he didn't feel nearly as vengeful and confident as he had during the morning. The only thing which drove him on was a stubborn determination not to lose the small advantage they had already gained.

'In any case,' he added, 'Shadroth might be badly injured. Remember how much blood there was on the hillside. He may hardly be capable of defending himself.'

'I doubt if he's that badly hurt,' Lea answered. 'He was still strong enough to get out from under all those rocks and make his way back to his lair. On the other hand, you may be right about not staying in the cave: we can't do anything if we hide in there.'

'I didn't say *you* shouldn't stay in the cave,' Tal said quickly. 'Only one of us need lie in wait for him; and I'm the only one who can't be harmed by the cold.'

But Lea dismissed the idea immediately.

'No,' she said firmly, 'I've already spent a whole night on my own, not knowing what was happening elsewhere. This time I'm coming with you.'

Her mind was so obviously made up that Tal didn't try to argue with her. Together, they spent the last hour of daylight preparing and eating a simple meal. Then, as the sun dropped down towards the distant hills, they left the cave and went several hundred paces along a path that led in the direction of Shadroth's lair.

By the time the evening shadow reached out across the Greenlands, they were crouched beside the Feln in the cover of thick undergrowth. Tal, all his senses alert, was listening for the noise of panic and flight which always signalled Shadroth's approach. As expected, the first warning bird calls echoed through the tree-tops not long after the sun had disappeared. But unlike previous occasions, they were not immediately followed by a rush of fleeing animals. A few large buck thundered along a near-by path, and that was all. It was as if most of the wild creatures had had ample time to avoid Shadroth. Also, beneath the few warning cries, there was another sound that Tal had never heard before: a slow, dragging noise, accompanied by the crash of falling trees. It took him a minute or two to identify its cause. The truth dawned on him quite suddenly: what he could hear was Shadroth himself as he dragged his huge bulk awkwardly through the dense vegetation. He was no longer a silent, menacing shadow, able to slide swiftly and easily between the trees. Over a period of many weeks he had taken physical shape and become totally a creature of flesh and bone – a creature whose enormous size was now a burden to him; and that, surely, could mean only one thing.

Tal stood up abruptly, a faint light of hope in his eyes.

'Listen,' he said, 'I think we must have hurt him quite badly.'

As he soon realized, speaking aloud like that was a mistake. Warned of their presence, Shadroth had stopped moving altogether, and for several minutes there was complete silence. They waited, expecting with each passing second to feel a cold blast of air on their faces; but it never arrived. And when at last the dragging noise began again, it came from a slightly different direction.

'Quick!' Tal cried, sensing a trap, 'he's trying to cut off our retreat to the cave.'

They all three ran headlong back towards the river: but when they rushed out onto the grassy bank that bordered the deep pool, there was no sign of Shadroth anywhere. Confused, they crept back into the cover of the trees, far enough away from the falls to be able to hear the sounds of the Greenlands clearly. The heavy dragging noise was still there, but was now far to the north, as if Shadroth were deliberately attempting to avoid them. More puzzled than scared, they ran through the fading twilight and clambered up the path beside the falls, reaching the top in time to see a dark shapeless hump struggle awkwardly across the upper shallows and disappear into the forest on the far bank.

'Perhaps he's frightened of the star-knife we've made,' Tal suggested hopefully.

But Lea was doubtful.

'It that's true,' she said, 'why did he keep clear of us on those other nights when we didn't have the star-knife? No, there's something else drawing him away – something far more important.'

'What could it be?' Tal wondered.

Lea turned away.

'I'm not sure,' she said in a worried voice, 'unless there's something happening at the Slopes.'

In silence, they slid back down the path beside the falls. For the time being, they could do nothing. To have followed Shadroth through the dark Greenlands would have been far too hazardous: even badly injured as he was, he was still capable of moving much more quickly than they. The only sensible course of action was to remain where they were and waylay Shadroth on his return shortly before dawn.

Fortunately, after their previous night's vigil, they slept soundly. Tal, curled up on the floor of the cave, close to the smouldering fire, had a dream so vivid that it was exactly like being possessed by the Gift – except that, in contrast to earlier visions, it was not dark or frightening. He was simply walking through the Greenlands in the bright morning sunlight. All around him the air was fresh and still, and there was a feeling of peace and tranquillity about the scene that reminded him of former happier days. Just ahead of him, he could see a small clearing. He knew that once he reached it, his fears and anxieties would fall away, everything would be as it had been in his early childhood. All he had to do was push past the final obstructing mass of undergrowth and step out into the open. He reached forward and clasped the thick, lush growth of leaves, but before he could draw them aside, someone grasped him firmly by the shoulders and began to shake him gently and persistently. He opened his eyes and, in the dim light from the fire, found himself staring at Lea's troubled face.

'What is it?' he asked, sitting up.

'It's the Feln,' she said, 'she's gone.'

'Left us, you mean?'

'Yes,' Lea answered. 'It's just one more thing I don't understand. She's always been there when we've needed her in the past. Why should she go now?'

'She might still come back,' Tal suggested.

'I don't think so,' Lea said. 'The sky's already greying. We should be out there on the watch. If she had meant to help us, she would be with us now.'

There was no time for further discussion. It was essential that they shouldn't miss Shadroth again, and together they climbed up to the shallows above the falls and waited. Slowly the arch of the sky became lighter, dispersing the deep shadows of the night. To the east, above the line of the Greenlands, a faint yellow halo grew steadily stronger. Soon the tip of the sun itself was showing; and minutes later Tal and Lea were standing drenched in its light. And yet throughout all that time they neither heard nor saw anything of Shadroth.

'He might have taken another route back to his lair,' Lea said.

But Tal was less sure. Recently, too much of Shadroth's behaviour had been unexplained, and Tal sensed that the time had come for them to stop guessing.

'There's only one way to find out,' he said.

And scrambling up the bank, he pushed his way through the dew-heavy bushes until he reached the base of an ancient tree, long since dead, that towered well over a hundred feet into the air. Its broad trunk had been scoured and pitted by the weather, offering him ample hand- and footholds, and, reaching up, he began the long climb. It took him several minutes to get clear of the tangle of vines and orchids that clung to the lower parts of the tree. Thereafter his progress was more rapid, and soon he was perched in the topmost branches, high above the coiling abundance of greenery. From there he could see far out over the wide plain. He looked first to the east, towards the tall cliffs and gentle Slopes where he had once lived – and immediately understood why they had not seen Shadroth blundering back across the river in the early dawn. Almost the whole of the scene before him was now bathed in warm yellow sunlight. Only one place, an area of the Greenlands near the bottom of the Slopes, was still sunk in shadow. Like a fragment of deepest night which had chosen to defy the day, it lingered broodingly amidst the bright morning.

As quickly as possible, Tal climbed back down the tree to where Lea was waiting.

'Could you see anything?' she asked.

'Shadroth hasn't returned to his lair,' he explained. 'He's still over by the Slopes, hiding in the cover of a thick grove of trees.'

'But it's daylight,' Lea said, surprised. 'You don't suppose he's too badly injured to get away?'

'I don't think so,' Tal answered. 'What you said last night is probably true. Something has been going on at the Slopes for some time. That's what has been drawing him away from us; it's what is holding him there now.'

Lea, unable to disguise the anxiety she was feeling, looked thoughtfully across the river.

'If that's so,' she said softly, 'they may need our help.'

'Don't forget that I'm an outcast there,' Tal reminded her. 'Kulok might kill me if I return.'

Lea ran one hand distractedly through her long hair.

'One of us could go,' she said. 'You could wait here while I find out what's happening.'

Tal shrugged, unsure of what to say.

'If you think it's best,' he murmured.

Lea placed a hand on his shoulder.

'We can't stay here while they're in danger,' she said. 'And I wouldn't be gone long. I might even be able to get back before nightfall.'

Again Tal didn't answer, and without another word she turned and began wading across the shallows.

Tal, watching her go, tried to assure himself that she would be all right. After all, what he had said was true: it was unsafe for him to return to the vicinity of the Slopes. But secretly he knew that was not his chief reason for remaining behind. There was another obstacle, waiting there for him in the thick cover of the trees. Ignoring it wouldn't make it go away – he was aware of that. Sooner or later, he and that dark shadow had to meet again. He alone bore Shadroth's mark on his forehead; he alone carried the star of deadly claws at his belt. And yet here he was allowing Lea to set out . . .

163

With sudden resolution, he slid down the bank and splashed his way through the shallows. He caught up with Lea just as she reached the far bank.

'I've been thinking,' he said lamely, 'I can hide in the Greenlands while you go up to the cave dwellings.'

His excuse sounded feeble and unconvincing in his own ears, but Lea smiled understandingly.

'It's probably safer for us to stay together,' was all she said.

In the hours that followed they ran steadily along the narrow, winding paths. By late in the morning they were in familiar surroundings, not far from the Slopes. Somewhere near by, Shadroth lay in wait; yet Tal, who was now leading the way, didn't slow down. What he was listening for was that deathly stillness which always betrayed Shadroth's presence. It came at last. They rounded a bend in the path and suddenly it was as if they were running through the land of the dead. There were no bird calls; there was no rustle of insects; even the light breeze had died away. Their footfalls, previously little more than a whisper on the soft carpet of loamy soil, now sounded deafening. Tal drew to a halt, breathing quickly, and looked around him. Murky shadows hung lifelessly beneath the branches of the trees, like hovering clouds of blue-black wood smoke. The sunlight itself had grown dim and muted, as though an unexpected twilight had settled on the land.

'Which direction should we take?' Lea whispered.

The shadows seemed to encroach on them from all sides, and Tal was about to admit that he was unsure when he was startled by a crackling in the undergrowth. They both whirled around, Tal groping frantically for the star-knife – but to their relief they found themselves staring into the familiar golden eyes of the Feln.

'So she didn't leave us after all,' Lea whispered happily. 'She's been waiting here for us all along.'

Apparently, that was exactly what she had been doing, because now the Feln turned purposefully and led the way through the sinister, unnatural twilight.

They followed her, moving as quietly as possible, constantly aware of the mass of cold darkness that lurked near by – fearing almost to glance behind in case they discovered those small glowing eyes observing them. They both knew that Shadroth must have sensed their presence by now and might rear up on the path before them at any moment. Yet as before, he chose to ignore them, all his evil attention concentrated elsewhere. Only once did they actually disturb him, when the Feln led them slightly too close to his hiding place. The dark shadows heaved outwards, carrying with them a breath of sickening cold. Momentarily, the dim sunlight flickered like a guttering candle. But they quickly moved away and the deathly stillness settled once again onto the Greenlands.

The brief detour could only have taken them four or five minutes, but to Tal it was like an age. When at last they emerged into the warmth and light he felt like shouting for joy.

'We did it!' he said triumphantly. 'We got past him!'

The Feln immediately glanced back at him, a hint of warning in her deep yellow eyes; and Lea held one finger to her lips.

'Hush,' she whispered, 'we can't be far from the Slopes now.'

Sure enough, there before them was the edge of the Greenlands. Through the hanging curtain of vines and leaves, Tal could see the soft green of the grassy Slopes and the towering fortress of the cliff. There had been a time when that sight had filled him with happiness, but so much had happened since then – and the cave dwellings, like the whole of the Greenlands, now inspired in him nothing more than a feeling of gloom and dread.

The Feln had already stopped. Stepping off the path, Tal crouched beside her, allowing Lea to pass.

'We'll wait here for two hours,' he said softly. 'If you haven't arrived by then, we'll return to the falls and come back tomorrow.'

Lea nodded and smiled encouragingly. Then, pushing aside the fringe of hanging growth, she disappeared from view.

Left to himself, Tal settled down to wait. Having successfully avoided Shadroth, he thought that he was probably secure for the time being – and yet he couldn't help feeling nervous, somehow exposed even there, within the cover of the Green-lands. It took him a minute or two to realize why he should feel like that: there had been no sound from up on the Slopes, no shouts of surprise or welcome at Lea's sudden appearance. It was almost as if the people of the Clan had been expecting her, had known of her arrival before she actually emerged into the open!

At that thought, Tal sprang to his feet. Beside him, the Feln was already growling a low warning. He saw her lips draw back, baring her long white canines, and an instant later she was gone, bounding away along the path. Tal tried to follow her, but he was not quick enough. Two hunters leaped out onto the path, barring his way; and before he could dodge aside, strong hands grabbed him from behind and threw him down onto his back. He heard a voice whisper angrily:

'It is just as Kulok said: the boy bears the evil mark upon him. He is the one who has brought Shadroth here by day.'

Tal looked up at the circle of hunters. They were men he had known from his earliest childhood, and yet not one of them showed him the slightest friendliness. To them, he was no more than an enemy. Grim-faced, star-knives held at the ready, they closed in on him from every side. As one of the men reached down to grasp him by the hair, he rolled over and tried to slide between the advancing feet. But again the hunters were too quick for him: his arms were pinned behind him and, despite his resistance, he was pushed out into the open. That was when his captors saw the black star of claws hanging from his belt.

'Look at what he carries!' someone said fearfully. 'Kulok must be told of this.'

Another voice answered:

'Kulok refuses to see or talk to anyone. You know that.'

'Yes, but this is different. He will break his silence when he hears that we have captured Shadroth's messenger.'

'No!' Tal cried out, 'you don't understand.'

But his protest achieved nothing. Shouting and struggling, he was dragged up the long grassy slope, past the look-out rock, to the foot of the cliffs. A crowd, attracted by the noise and excitement, had already gathered outside the dwellings. Among them was Nator, who now rushed to Tal's assistance.

'Release the boy!' he cried. 'He has done you no harm.'

He was about to throw his arms protectively around Tal when all at once he noticed the jet-black scar on his grandson's forehead. Immediately he fell back, a look of uncertainty on his old face.

'What is it?' he asked in a low voice.

'He is the creature of Shadroth,' one of the hunters said harshly.

'No,' Tal replied, 'I am his enemy. This is the mark of his anger – nothing else.'

'Kulok shall be the judge of that,' the hunter said.

Before Tal could reply, he was forced up the steep ramp towards the Council Chamber. At the low doorway, the youngest of the hunters, whom Tal now recognized as Galt's son, beat the wooden drum which stood beside the opening.

'We have captured Tal, son of Norn,' he called out. 'He bears on him the mark and weapons of Shadroth.'

There was a brief silence before Kulok's voice, from within the chamber, called out the single word of command:

'Enter.'

Instantly, Tal's arms were released and he was pitched forward through the low doorway. It took him a few moments to accustom his eyes to the half-light. The first thing he noticed was Lea standing quietly against the side wall. She shook her head at him in a way he didn't understand and pointed to the far end of the chamber. There, on a raised half-circle of rock, was Kulok. He was sitting cross-legged, dressed only in a loincloth. His hair was unbound and fell forward over his face in long black curls. Before him, spread out on the floor, was his golden cloak – and in the middle of the cloak, squatting there like a malignant black toad, was the evil charm, its pinpricks of eyes gleaming in the shadows.

As Tal stepped forward, Kulok raised his head. In the gloom at the end of the chamber, it was impossible to make out his expression.

'The time has come,' was all he said.

20. Under Siege

Tal moved defensively back towards the door.

'The time has come for what?' he asked nervously.

But to his amazement, there was nothing aggressive about Kulok's attitude. His former arrogance and impatience had disappeared entirely. Rising to his feet, he stepped carefully around the cloak and came over to where Tal and Lea were standing.

'It is time', he said firmly, 'to banish the evil to the darkness from whence it came.'

He pointed, as he spoke, to the charm which sat like a blob of immovable shadow on the soft gold of the cloak.

'You mean take it back to the cave behind the falls?' Lea said in an astonished voice.

Kulok nodded and hung his head.

'But what made you change your mind?' Lea asked.

'It was that day when we met in the Greenlands,' he explained. 'Up until then I told myself that Tal was to blame for everything. But after our meeting it was different, almost . . . almost like an awakening. It's hard to explain. You see, when the stone from Tal's sling struck the charm I . . . I felt Shadroth move, just as though he were inside me – as though he were lodged here in my own skull. He was miles away, but still I felt him move. Somehow he and the charm were connected. There was no denying it. And I was the bearer of the charm – Shadroth's messenger. Nobody else. Not you, nor Tal, nor any other member of the Clan. Just me. From then on, I knew that I was the one to blame, that I was the bringer of evil. I had disrupted the law of the Greenlands, given the land over to futile death and destruction, and so called Shadroth forth from the earth as surely as if he had crawled from a dark hollow in my own mind.'

There was a brief silence. Tal could hear the hunters outside the chamber shuffling their feet on the stone ramp.

'Why didn't you take the charm back to the falls as soon as you realized the truth?' Lea asked.

Kulok looked from his sister to Tal, and then down at the floor.

'That, too, is hard to explain,' he murmured. 'Once you have worn the charm, it is no easy thing to give it up. Casting it off is like . . . like cutting out a part of your own mind. Since our last meeting in the Greenlands, I have spoken to no one. I have sat here in the chamber alone, wrestling with the dark voice inside me, which has never ceased whispering its promises. It has taken me until now to muster enough courage and determination to come to a decision.'

Tal, who had been listening with growing excitement, stepped closer to the young chieftain.

'You say you realized that the charm was evil,' he said intently. 'But when exactly did you begin to consider taking it back to the cave behind the falls?'

'Immediately after speaking to you and Lea in the Greenlands,' Kulok answered.

Tal glanced meaningfully at Lea. There was no need for words between them: they both understood now why Shadroth had chosen to come to the Slopes night after night rather than follow them. It had been Kulok, not their puny efforts, which had posed the greatest threat to his continued existence. As Argalna had warned them back there in the Grasslands, Shadroth could always sense the presence of any danger to himself.

'And when did you actually make the decision to give the charm up?' Tal added. 'Was it just as I walked into the chamber?'

'I came to a decision last night,' Kulok said. 'Shortly before dawn, I took the charm from around my neck and placed it on the cloak.'

Again Tal looked at Lea: it was clear to them both why

Shadroth, despite his injuries and his hatred of the sunlight, had not returned to his lair: he had realized that his existence in the Greenlands was threatened; that unless he was on his guard, he would be banished to the grave-like earth from which he had come.

'But the moment I saw Shadroth lurking outside,' Kulok went on, 'my courage failed me. I have been watching since dawn, hoping that he would leave and allow me to creep down into the Greenlands unseen.'

'Then what did you mean a few minutes ago, when you said the time had come?' Lea asked, puzzled.

'When you both entered the chamber, I felt ashamed,' Kulok admitted. 'Here was I, cowering in safety, while you had successfully crossed the Greenlands and crept past the waiting Shadroth. I understood that the time had come for me to set out. The charm must be returned, regardless of the consequences. What right have I to delay any longer? Who was it who hunted the Feln and took the charm from its rightful place? Who lured Shadroth from his sombre dwelling deep in the earth? It is not you, but I, who must go out and face him.'

Kulok, his sense of shame written clearly on his handsome features, half turned away, but Tal reached out and touched him gently on the shoulder.

'You are not wholly to blame,' he said softly. 'I must also bear part of the guilt. There is one other thing that Argalna told us: he said that the charm on its own is not enough to raise Shadroth. He does not appear until someone has painted his likeness. And I am the one who did that. You saw my painting yourself, down there on the look-out rock. It is you and I together who woke Shadroth. He found his own dark image reflected in our minds and so he rose to challenge us.'

Kulok took Tal's hand in both of his and squeezed it lightly.

'You have no cause to befriend me now,' he said humbly, 'not after the unjust way I have treated you.'

'I tell you only what I believe to be the truth,' Tal replied.

'And I thank you for it,' Kulok said, his tone revealing his gratitude even more clearly than the words themselves. 'Yet still most of the guilt is mine, and I must answer for it.'

With that, he walked resolutely across the cavern to where the cloak lay spread out on the floor. Before stooping to pick up the charm, he paused, hesitating just for a second or two. In that brief interval, an ominous hush seemed to settle on the chamber. Tal recognized it at once: it was the same unearthly silence that always revealed Shadroth's presence. He wanted to shout out a warning, but already Kulok's fingers were closing around the hideous blackness of the charm. And as they did so, the stillness of the Greenlands was torn by a terrible howl of rage and despair.

Tal spun around in time to see the two hunters who had been waiting on the ramp scurry through the doorway and flatten themselves against the side walls. From outside, there came faint cries of fear and dismay. Both Tal and Lea, with Kulok close behind them, leaped towards the opening and peered out.

Again the stillness was rent by a demented howl. It came from the area of brooding shadow just inside the Greenlands. Immediately afterwards, as though in response to his own cry, Shadroth moved. The darkness surrounding him stirred uneasily, bringing giant trees and ferns crashing to the ground; and slowly Shadroth's huge bulk rose into view, a creature from a nightmare world rising up to defy the daylight. The very sun's rays seemed to draw back from him, unwilling to penetrate the circle of darkness which enshrouded his vast shapeless body. Within that particular circle, he remained what he had always been: a shaggy demon of the night; a brutal destructive urge that had somehow escaped from the deepest, most hidden recesses of the earth. Like some dream figure come to wreak vengeance on those who had created him, he rose now to his full height: terrifying, deathly cold, vindictive, intent on seeking out all who dared to pit themselves against him.

As Tal watched, almost hypnotized by what he saw, Shadroth lumbered forward, tearing a jagged path through the Greenlands. At the foot of the Slopes he stopped and looked directly up at the Council Chamber in which Tal and Kulok now sheltered. Even in the bright sunlight those small eyes glowed fiercely, blood-red pools which conveyed the promise of death and spoke clearly of the terrible hatred that Shadroth harboured for these two people upon whom he was forced to rely – who had once summoned him from the darkness and who now threatened his continued existence.

Before him, on the lower portion of the Slopes, the milk-white cattle stood transfixed. With a single heave of his body, Shadroth smashed two of them to the ground. Only then did the others break and run, hobbling away on stiff legs as they struggled to free their limbs and joints from the deadly cold that threatened to freeze them to the spot. As they staggered clear, Shadroth again urged his massive body into ungainly motion, his forward progress crushing the already mangled bodies of the two dead cattle. He barely noticed them: to him, they were mere obstacles, like stones or trees. All his vicious energy was directed at the single chamber in the cliffside, where his protective charm and his sworn enemies waited.

Terrified though he was, Tal could see how badly Shadroth was injured. One whole side of his body sagged, dragging on the ground, encumbering him as he moved. Yet even in that condition, his power and strength were formidable. As he surged up the Slopes, his shaggy coat rippled dully, spasms of enormous energy shuddering through him, driving him ever faster. His gleaming eyes now conveyed a fanatical sense of purpose, never wavering, riveted on a single target in the whole breadth and height of the cliff.

It was Kulok who first guessed at his mad purpose.

'Get back!' he yelled.

He, the hunters, Tal, and Lea, all scrambled towards the far end of the cave. Before they could reach it, Shadroth slammed into the cliff, sending them sprawling to the floor. All around them, the stone walls trembled and groaned; and above their heads, long uneven cracks appeared in the solid rock of the ceiling. After that there was silence. Carefully, Tal rose to his knees and then slowly stood upright – only to be thrown down once more as Shadroth again hurled himself against the face of the cliff.

Four times in all he charged the unyielding stone. Unable

to penetrate the narrow opening of the chamber, he seemed determined to destroy the tiny cavern in which his enemies lay hidden. At his final attempt, it felt almost as though he had succeeded. Slabs of rock fell from the walls and ceiling and dust filled the air. Tal thought for a moment that the whole cliff was sliding down on top of them; but when the dust settled, the chamber was still intact. Hardly daring to breathe, he braced himself for the next juddering blow; and only when the passing seconds had lengthened into minutes did he relax and sit up.

His companions were unhurt. One by one, bewildered and frightened, they stood up and surveyed the wreckage all around them. Taking care not to make a sound, Tal crept to the door and looked down onto the Slopes. Shadroth had retired to a point midway between the look-out rock and the edge of the Greenlands. Resting there on the grass, squat and strangely formless, his eyes glowing with suppressed malice, he appeared more dreadful than ever. His attack on the cliff had obviously injured him further: the damaged side of his body drooped brokenly; and from somewhere within its hairy mass, great drops of black blood splashed onto the ground and ran in narrow rivulets down the hillside. Yet still he was far from defeated – at the slightest sound, his eyes would flash and his whole enormous body start into life.

Watching him, Tal knew instinctively that the struggle was not yet over, nor would it be until Shadroth was banished from the Greenlands or utterly destroyed. There was a furtive movement behind him and Kulok and Lea joined him at the doorway.

'Do you think he'll give up if we remain in hiding?' Lea whispered hopefully.

'He's fighting for his very existence,' he said. 'He won't give up easily. If necessary, he may even starve us out.'

The idea of remaining cooped up for days was a bleak prospect and from then on nobody spoke very much. Slowly the hours dragged by. In the middle of the afternoon, clouds gathered overhead and it began to rain steadily. For a time they were hopeful that the rain might drive Shadroth away; but their hope was short-lived. Grunting with discontent, he merely huddled closer to the hillside as though settling himself for a long unpleasant vigil. Occasionally he shuddered slightly as the rain, freezing instantly on contact with his shaggy coat, tumbled from his sides in a fine cascade of flashing crystals. But apart from that he remained immovable.

By early evening Kulok had begun to pace restlessly backwards and forwards across the width of the chamber.

'We can't just hide here doing nothing!' he burst out at last. 'There must be some means of escape, some way of getting to the falls.'

Tal was leaning against the wall, his eyes closed, listening to the gentle rustle of the rain outside.

'There's no way out of here,' he said quietly, 'not now.'

He thought he was voicing what they all knew, but to his surprise Lea disagreed.

'No,' she said in a low voice, 'there is still one possibility.'

Tal opened his eyes, and Kulok abruptly stopped his pacing.

'We can still try using a decoy,' Lea went on. 'If one of us lured Shadroth away, you, Kulok, could run for the cover of the Greenlands. With Shadroth injured, you might be able to get to the falls ahead of him.'

'But how is it possible to lure him anywhere?' Tal asked. 'As soon as anyone steps down there onto the Slopes, Shadroth will destroy him.'

'Then don't go onto the Slopes,' Lea answered. 'Go up, onto the cliffs above.'

'Yes,' Kulok said eagerly, a glimmer of hope appearing in his deep-set eyes. 'If someone went up the ramp to the broad ledges above, he could then climb the stone stairway to the path which runs along the face of the cliff. Once up there, he would be safe, because the path soon becomes so narrow that Shadroth would be unable to follow. Still, it would be hazardous, because it is a steep climb and there is no further shelter beyond this chamber.'

'It's worth a try, though,' Lea said, jumping to her feet.

But Kulok placed a detaining hand on her shoulder.

'You have already done enough to help the Clan,' he said. 'It would be better for one of the hunters to go.'

He glanced across at Galt's son, who was standing pale-faced and frightened at the side of the cavern; but before he could speak, Tal moved quickly towards the door.

'There is only one person who should undertake such a task,' he said. He tried to make himself sound firm and decisive, though in fact he had never felt less confident in his life. 'I am small enough to crawl out along the narrow path; and I alone can resist Shadroth's cold. Also, I am not helpless' – and here he patted the star of black claws which he still carried. 'If Shadroth corners me, he will feel the bite of his own deathly touch.'

'Let me at least come with you,' Lea pleaded. 'We've stayed together so far. Now is not the time to part.'

'No,' Tal said in the same decisive tone. 'Your courage is needed elsewhere. If Kulok sets out alone, he can expect no help from the Feln. But if you go with him, the Feln may guide you quickly and safely to the falls. In the darkness, and with Shadroth close behind, you will have need of her sharp eyes.'

Kulok, his face working with emotion, came over and placed his hands on Tal's shoulders.

'I have no words to express my gratitude,' he said in a choked voice. 'I pray only that the spirit of the Feln may carry you to safety.'

He stepped back and Tal turned to peer outside. It was dusk and the rain continued to fall. He had a sudden irrational desire to see the sunlight once again, but he knew that was impossible. As Kulok had suggested earlier, there could be no further delay. And without even a word of farewell, he ducked through the doorway and began sprinting up the ramp.

Before he had taken more than five strides, Shadroth's death cry sounded from the Slopes. As always, it sent shivers of apprehension up his spine, but still he didn't falter. Lowering his head, ignoring the fine rain which struck chill on his exposed skin, he drove himself even faster, putting out all his strength in a desperate bid to reach the safety of the heights.

Far below him, he heard a dragging noise as Shadroth forced his huge body into motion. Shortly afterwards, the ramp trembled under Tal's feet and he slipped on the wet surface and fell. Glancing back, he saw that Shadroth had reached the ramp and was lumbering up after him, his red eyes boring through the growing dusk, glowing now with the anticipation of success. That dreadful sight only hardened Tal's resolve and he leaped up and ran as he never had before. Ahead of him, through the fine drizzle, he could see the top of the ramp. Once there, he would have a reasonable chance of survival – and with that hope to urge him on, he forced his flagging body over the remaining distance.

Gasping for breath, his heart pounding in his ears, he burst out onto the first of the broad ledges. Beyond this level, up a giant step of twenty feet or more, was a further ledge which ended in a sheer stone wall. In that direction, Tal knew, lay certain death. His task now was to locate the stone stairway which led up to the narrow path. In the uncertain light of growing dusk, he stumbled forward, searching for the steps which would carry him beyond Shadroth's grasp. Although he had never climbed them before, he knew they were located approximately halfway along the ledge. Yet to his dismay, when he drew near the spot, he could see nothing but a vertical wall of rock – nothing more. For a few moments he thought he must be imagining things and he groped frantically at the hard rocky surface. It was only then that he noticed the jagged fissure in the wall slightly to his left, and below it a tumbled heap of stone.

In a flash, he understood what had happened. During Shadroth's insane assault upon the cliff, the staircase had broken away from the inner side of the ledge and fallen down, smashing itself to pieces. There was no longer any possibility of reaching the upper path: he was trapped out in the open.

21. Last Stand

Somehow, Tal managed not to give way to panic. Behind him he could hear Shadroth hurrying up the ramp and he knew that he had very little time left. His duty now was to ensure that Kulok had as much of a start as possible and to do that he must sell his life dearly. Only in that way could he delay Shadroth and so help the Clan.

Oddly enough, that realization served to calm him. This, after all, was the end of his struggle – and faced with the inevitable, he looked coolly around him, assessing the situation. The upper path was out of the question, as was all thought of retreating back down the ramp. His one chance was to scale the giant step and make a stand at the far end of the second of the two ledges. That strategy alone could not save him, but it would put off the end for a few more minutes; and as he fully realized, every minute was vital to the future of the Greenlands.

The problem was how to reach that upper ledge. The smooth vertical step could not be climbed, but over near the edge of the cliff, not far from where he now stood, a gaunt and ancient tree grew from the thin soil that had gathered in a deep crack in the rock. The outermost limbs of that tree arched over towards the high step, and there was a faint possibility that he could jump from one of those limbs onto the second ledge. It would be a long and desperate leap – he recognized that – but at this stage he had nothing to lose.

As this simple plan formed in his mind, a faint smile spread across his face – for he suddenly remembered one of the paintings that Argalna had shown him. It had been the last one he had looked at and had depicted him crouched in a tree, staring at the advancing figure of Shadroth. Like so many events during the past weeks, this one too had been foreseen. And after this?

But Shadroth was nearing the top of the ramp; the warning pain in Tal's forehead was throbbing insistently; and already he could feel the air around him growing colder. With a last look at the darkening Greenlands, he ran over to the tree and, grasping one of the lower limbs, pulled himself up amongst the sparse foliage. From there, he saw Shadroth's murky form appear above the surface of the ledge. For a moment or two the creature stopped, bewildered by the unexpected disappearance of his enemy, his tiny eyes searching every corner. Tal, aware that he would not remain undetected for long, used those few moments well. Moving as silently as he could, and taking advantage of every inch of cover, he climbed up to one of the out-thrusting limbs. From that point onwards, he had to rely solely on balance. Ignoring the sheer drop on one side, his arms held out straight, he walked slowly along the gnarled limb.

Almost immediately, Shadroth spotted him, and with a howl of rage came surging across the ledge. The cold blast of his breath struck Tal while he was still only halfway along the limb and he swayed dangerously from side to side; but still he continued to walk slowly forward, his eyes fixed on the vertical thrust of the cliff. Not until the thin outer portion of the branch was bending under him did he stop and look down. What he saw appalled him. The gap between the end of the branch and the upper ledge had appeared wide when he had observed it from below. Now it was like a vast unbridgeable gulf. Behind him, he heard Shadroth howl once more, and he gathered himself for a desperate leap. Yet try as he might, he could not force himself to jump. Even his fear of Shadroth was not sufficient to make him leap to his own death, and he remained where he was, half-crouched, frozen in space and time.

It was at that instant that Shadroth reached the base of the tree and struck it a vicious blow. With a groaning and splintering of timber, it toppled forward, more than half its roots torn out of the thin soil. Caught unawares, Tal was catapulted into the air. With a cry of horror, he closed his eyes and braced himself for the long sickening fall. But instead of dropping down and down to the Slopes below, he was suddenly caught by the thin upper branches of the tree. The twigs and rough bark scratched and tore at his skin, but they held him, saving him from that terrible drop.

Had Shadroth chosen then to strike the tree another blow, Tal would certainly have plummeted to his death. What saved him was Shadroth's hesitation. Perhaps the huge creature was distracted by the falling rain or by the pain of his own injuries. Whatever the reason, he momentarily lost sight of his prey and he paused and peered over the edge of the cliff, probably expecting to see Tal's shattered body spread out on the ground hundreds of feet below. That brief pause was the opportunity that Tal needed. The angle at which the tree was now leaning took it much closer to the upper ledge; and Tal, quickly disentangling himself from the smaller twigs and branches, ran along the nearest limb and leaped out into space.

He landed heavily on the upper step, rolled over once, and scrambled to his feet. Thirty paces away was the vertical wall of stone which cut off all further retreat. He reached it in a dozen strides and flattened himself against it, already pulling at the cord which secured the star of claws to his belt.

Meanwhile Shadroth, frustrated yet again, screamed with rage and charged towards the tall step which divided the two ledges. All that prevented his clearing it at a single bound was the sinister black star which Tal now held in his hand. At the sight of those five tapered claws, he veered away from the step and drew back. For perhaps a full minute, there was no other sound but the gentle whisper of the rain and the hoarse rasping of Shadroth's icy breath. Tal, aware that this was only a temporary delay, dropped down onto one knee and steadied himself for what must follow. His forehead ached and he shook his head to clear his vision. He would have only one chance with the star-knife and he had to make the most of it. Strangely calm, he looked into the baleful eyes of his enemy, of this creature which he and Kulok had brought into being. The redness of those eyes seemed to intensify for a fraction of a second and he knew the charge was about to begin. But just as

Shadroth strained forward, a cry rang out from the head of the ramp:

'Shadroth!'

His concentration broken, Tal looked past Shadroth to where Kulok was standing at the far end of the lower ledge. He was again wearing the Feln cloak which was closed at the front and reached from his shoulders to the ground. Except for his face, the only part of him that was unprotected by the Feln skin was his right hand and arm, and these were thrust out before him.

'Do you dare to face this?' Kulok shouted.

And only then did Tal notice what he was holding: dangling from his clenched fist was the black charm.

'No, Kulok!' he shouted. 'That belongs in the cave behind the falls! Not here!'

But it was too late now for either protests or regret. Shadroth had already turned and seen the charm, and immediately Tal and the star of claws were forgotten. Here at last was both a victim and the promise of eternal security. Swinging his damaged body around, he lumbered back along the ledge, sidling past Kulok so that the young chieftain could not retreat down the ramp. Then, slowly and deliberately, he closed in on his prey.

Tal, watching from the upper ledge, saw the ice forming on the folds of the Feln cloak. As Kulok gradually gave ground, his movements became more stiff and ungainly. Rendered half-senseless by the terrible cold, he blundered backwards to the very edge of the cliff. One foot actually slid into space before he recovered himself and stood trembling and helpless before his enemy. Now, he could no longer move: his arm was fixed rigidly before him; his face was frozen into an expression of horror. Shadroth, victory within his grasp, towered triumphantly above his victim.

But before he could deliver that final crushing blow, Tal hurled the star of claws directly at the blazing red eyes. He heard the razor edges slicing through hair and flesh and bone – and then he was down on the ground, both hands over his ears, trying to blot out the tearing, piercing scream which rose echoing from the surrounding walls of stone. As the unearthly noise died away, he looked up: through the twilight and the driving rain, he saw the hump of darkness that was Shadroth spin slowly round and topple off the edge of the cliff.

He didn't hear the great body hit the ground. He was already clambering down onto the lower level and running over to where Kulok was lying pale and frozen upon the bare rock. As he reached him, Lea too appeared at the top of the ramp.

'Is he still alive?' she burst out, struggling for breath after the long climb.

'I think so,' Tal replied, 'but we have no time to lose.'

Between them, they dragged Kulok across the ledge and some distance down the ramp, to where they were met by several members of the Clan led by Nator.

'Thank goodness you're safe!' the old man cried joyfully, hugging his young grandson.

'It's not me you have to worry about now,' Tal said, gently pulling free, 'it's Kulok. He needs warmth and shelter if he's to survive.'

Nator looked at the frozen body and quickly signalled for two of the hunters to carry the young chieftain to the dwellings. As he followed the men down the ramp, he said sadly:

'This is how my own son died.' His voice was almost choked with tears. With an effort, he regained his composure and added more grimly: 'Shadroth will pay for what he has done this day.'

'He has paid already,' Tal explained. 'His body lies broken down there on the Slopes.'

But to his surprise, both Nator and Lea shook their heads.

'I wish with all my heart that what you say were true,' Nator murmured, 'but I was here on the ramp when the body fell. I saw it strike the ground. And I tell you now, Shadroth is still alive.'

'But that's impossible!' Tal protested.

He looked questioningly at Lea, hoping that she would deny what Nator had just said – only to read in her eyes the same unwelcome news.

'I also saw him fall,' she said in a subdued voice. 'He lay still only for a moment before crawling off into the Greenlands.'

'So all this has been for nothing!' Tal said desperately.

'No, not for nothing,' Lea corrected him. 'The enmity between you and Kulok is over. Kulok went to your rescue instead of journeying to the falls; he couldn't bear to leave you in such danger. He said that would have been the worst betrayal of all.'

'And is this the reward for his kindness?' Tal asked bitterly, pointing to the stiff figure carried by the hunters.

'He knew the chance he was taking,' Lea said softly.

'No!' Tal almost shouted – and suddenly he was filled with an overwhelming sense of urgency. 'His courage will be repaid as it deserves. What he has done will not come to nothing!'

Running ahead, he stopped the hunters and made them lower the chieftain to the ground. Kulok's right hand was still tightly closed and Tal had to prise it open in order to slip the charm and its cord from between the fingers.

'We shall see now whether Shadroth lives,' he said, grasping the charm in his own clenched fist.

'Don't be a fool!' Nator said. 'The rain has stopped and it's almost dark. This is not the time to challenge Shadroth.'

But he was pleading with the empty air. Tal was already at the end of the ramp, running past the dimly lit dwellings, past the look-out rock, and down the long grass-covered slope. At the edge of the Greenlands, he paused briefly and whistled twice. Shortly afterwards, there was a rustling in the undergrowth and the familiar outline of the Feln slid from the shadows.

'We have one last journey to make,' he whispered, and held the charm up for the Feln to see.

She immediately snarled and flattened her ears, but she also understood what was expected of her. With a swish of her tail, she turned and loped off into the gloom, with Tal following close behind.

After the strain of the day, that long run through the Greenlands proved a tiring journey for Tal. What made it particularly exhausting was the charm itself, which seemed to grow heavier all the time. With each passing mile, its dull weight dragged at his arm, jolting his shoulder until it hurt. Once, when he stopped to rest, he imagined that a voice was whispering inside his head, telling him to hang the cord around his neck where it would not encumber him. But he had seen what effect the wearing of the charm had had on Kulok and he resisted the temptation. Tired though he was, he was alert to the hidden power of the thing he carried; he was aware that there could be no safety and no rest for him until it was imprisoned once more behind the protective veil of the falls.

The act of placing the charm within its dark niche – that, he knew, would be the final test. Shadroth would not suffer defeat without a last desperate struggle. Tal felt sure that he was waiting somewhere in the Greenlands, watching for an opportunity to strike out and retrieve the charm. But where? – that was the question.

During the first few hours, Tal was forever listening for the deathly stillness that accompanied Shadroth. But as the night wore on, a faint hope began to stir inside him. Perhaps after all Shadroth had given up; perhaps he had been so badly crippled that he had dragged his shattered body back to the safety of the mountain lair. As his optimism grew, Tal quickened his pace, and soon after midnight he detected the roar of the falls. Never had he been more glad to hear any sound.

'We shall see whether Shadroth lives,' he murmured once again.

Yet no sooner had he uttered those prophetic words than the all-too-familiar pain in his forehead began to throb out a warning; and immediately he understood where Shadroth had chosen to make his final stand.

The moon was directly overhead when he reached the deep pool. With the Feln beside him, he crept out of the thick undergrowth and looked longingly at the cascade of falling water. It was tantalizingly close, and yet so far away – for between himself and the edge of the pool was the giant figure of Shadroth, hunched over, brooding on his own pain. Tal thought for a moment that the monstrous creature had its back to them, because he could not see the burning red eyes. He was soon to realize his error. As he inched forward, Shadroth suddenly reared up, barring his way, and he saw then why the eyes had not been visible. They no longer existed. Where they had once glowed fiercely, there was now a tunnel of everlasting night. Shadroth was blind, his eyes torn away by his own savage claws.

For the second time since leaving the Slopes, Tal's spirits rose. Here, at last, was real cause for hope. What did it matter if Shadroth still possessed the strength of a hundred men? Without his sight, he was helpless. Rashly, Tal stole silently towards the edge of the pool – and very nearly lost his life. For with a roar that shattered the calm of the night, Shadroth lashed out, tearing up a great swathe of earth less than a foot from where Tal crouched.

Hastily, he drew back into the cover of the trees. He could now see how Shadroth had detected his whereabouts. Even the slightest movement by him or the Feln caused the huge sightless head to rise and test the breeze; and always, immediately afterwards, the dark shapeless body would face squarely in their direction.

Here, then, was the same stalemate as he had encountered at the Slopes, with Shadroth effectively in control – or so Tal thought. But he had reckoned without the Feln. Silent, almost docile until now, she suddenly uttered a deep growl and charged directly towards her ancient enemy. Like a blur of gold in the pale moonlight, she sped across the wet grass and sprang straight at the hulking shadow that had oppressed the Greenlands for so long. Yet for all her speed, Shadroth was faster, in spite of his injuries; and had he possessed his sight, that moment would have been the Feln's last. As it was, guided by scent and sound alone, he struck her only a glancing blow – though even that was enough to knock her aside and send her rolling helplessly towards the trees.

Forgetful of his own safety, Tal rushed over to where she lay. She was not seriously hurt, merely stunned, and he tugged at the loose skin of her neck, trying to urge her to her feet. Groggily, she staggered up, and immediately fell again.

'You have to get up!' he whispered urgently.

Already Shadroth was moving towards them. Locked within his own darkness, he was hesitant at first, unsure of himself; but with each shuffling step he gained in confidence. Desperately, Tal pulled at the soft golden fur. Again she half-rose, only to stagger and fall panting on the grass, her beautiful head lolling from side to side as she struggled to throw off her dizziness. Tal glanced up. Shadroth was almost upon them. And suddenly it dawned on him that he was about to lose her; after all that she had done for him, she was going to be destroyed by Shadroth.

Somehow, that simple truth appeared more terrible to him than anything that had happened so far. Even before it had occurred, he wanted to weep for this friend who was as dear to him as Lea. All that prevented him from breaking down there and then was his sense of outrage. The injustice of it! That she should die like this! Pointlessly! When they had been so close to victory! And he, Tal, could do nothing . . . nothing . . .

It was then, faced with the inevitability of the Feln's death, that Tal perceived what should have been obvious to him all along. This, after all, was where everything had begun, where he, too, had had an almost fatal encounter with Shadroth; and this was where it must end. Now!

Raising his head, he looked up at the looming shadow which was so close that it blotted out half the starlit sky.

'Shadroth!' he shouted, just as Kulok had done from the top of the ramp.

The very abruptness of that cry made Shadroth falter, and that was his undoing. Tal had already slipped the black sling from his belt and was scrabbling in his leather pouch. His fingers closed on the fragment of claw which Shadroth himself had implanted in his forehead so many weeks before. Placing it in the cup of the sling, he whirled it swiftly above his head and sent it straight at the place where those deadly eyes had once gleamed with malice.

He knew that such a tiny fragment would not stop Shadroth for long; but all he needed was a second or two, time enough to reach the lip of the pool. With the cord of the charm clamped between his teeth, he darted forward; and as Shadroth screamed and staggered back, he passed beneath the groping arms, actually brushing the icy fur, and dived head first from the top of the bank. While he was still in mid air, he felt Shadroth's freezing breath close around him – and then he was sinking deep beneath the surface, swimming through the warm darkness.

Halfway across the pool, he came up for air, breaking through the thin film of ice which now covered the surface. Above him, the stars had disappeared altogether, obliterated by the evil black form which strained towards him from the bank. Taking a full breath, he dived again, determined not to come up until he had gained the safety of the cave. With his lungs bursting, he reached the turbulent water directly beneath the falls and immediately began to angle upwards. But while he was still some feet beneath the surface, something hard and unyielding struck him on the side, gashing him badly and sending him spinning back down into the depths. The force and unexpectedness of that blow drove the air from his lungs in a rush, and involuntarily he breathed in water. Instantly, he was fighting for his life, clawing his way through a hail of buffeting blows that drained his body of its remaining strength. Lost and bewildered in the darkness, his outstretched hands encountered the rough face of a rock wall and he clung to it, pulling himself upwards hand over hand. Somehow, half-drowned and bleeding from a number of wounds, he reached the surface and crawled feebly out onto the floor of the cave.

Behind him, the falls was no longer a cascade of foaming water: it had been transformed into a sheet of solid ice, buckling and cracking into jagged pieces that crashed down into the pool. Dimly, he understood that it was those large pieces of ice which had nearly killed him – they had been Shadroth's last despairing attempt to save himself. Even now, he continued to howl and scream out there in the night, beating himself relentlessly against the one door through which he could not pass.

Summoning the last of his strength, Tal crawled slowly across the darkened cave. He was too tired and battered to feel any joy. He knew only that he had to locate the niche in the wall and free himself of this evil which had plagued him for so long. At the very edge of total exhaustion, he blundered into the wall and felt along it until he found the shallow, flat-bottomed depression. Then he took the cord from between his teeth and placed the charm back in its obscure shrine.

After that he lay down on the floor, his eyes closed. Outside, Shadroth's frantic cries became steadily weaker and more distant. As they receded into the night, Tal's whole body began to shake with cold. But he was already losing consciousness and nothing seemed to matter any longer. All he really wanted was to sleep, and with a sigh he rolled over onto his side and curled up. He failed to hear the last of Shadroth's cries; nor did he experience the deep silence that settled onto the Greenlands – not that deathly stillness he had learned to dread, but the silence of peace and rest.

22. Belonging

It was Lea who found him in the cave. By then, he was suffering badly from exposure and loss of blood. For several days he remained unconscious, teetering between life and death; but gradually his youth and natural strength began to exert themselves and he ceased to be in danger.

He awoke for the first time on the fourth day and tried unsuccessfully to sit up.

'Lie still,' Nator said, and he pushed him gently back onto the couch.

Lea was also in the room, her face a picture of happiness.

'Shadroth has gone,' she said, speaking with a rush, 'and Kulok is alive, and the mark on your forehead is fading. As soon as you're well . . .'

But he didn't hear the rest: he was already drifting back into sleep.

When he next awoke, he felt strong enough to take a little food; and within a few days he was sitting up and talking. From then on, his improvement was rapid. At the end of a week he could stagger shakily over to the door; and despite Nator's protests, he insisted on going outside.

He and Kulok recuperated together. Once such bitter enemies, there was now a strange bond of friendship between them. In the bright mornings, they would sit out on the grassy hillside, their backs against the look-out rock, and talk quietly of all that had happened to them. It was to Tal that Kulok first confided his intention of giving up the role of chieftain.

'There's no need to do that,' Tal argued. 'You have made up for the mistakes of the past.'

But Kulok disagreed.

'The Clan will be better off without a chieftain,' he insisted.

'The Council can rule far more wisely than any individual. Also, a whole Council would never give way to the madness which possessed me.'

Kulok's decision, once made, had a marked effect upon him: his dark and gloomy memories of the past seemed to lose their hold upon his mind, and he grew steadily more cheerful. Watching him laughing and talking with Lea, Tal found it difficult not to envy him; for try as he might, he, Tal, could not shake off the gloom of the past. Although Shadroth no longer existed, banished to the unknown darkness from which he had so mysteriously emerged, his brooding presence somehow continued to affect Tal's vision of the Greenlands. Time and again he told himself that he was being foolish: Shadroth was gone; it was only the bitterness of memory which dimmed the bright sunlight and gave a sinister quality to the sparkling green of tree and vine. But that knowledge made no difference to the way he felt. In his eyes, the Greenlands had become a place of destruction, and he longed to leave it.

More and more, he found himself thinking of the Grasslands and of the time he had spent with the Gentle Folk. No darkness existed there, no violence or threat; each day had been filled with light and laughter. Sitting alone on the hillside, gazing at the distant mountains, he felt sure that he could never recapture such an experience here. Not now. The only solution was to set out along the river as he had done once before.

Lea was probably the only one who understood how deeply troubled he was, and with her usual keen perception she guessed at the true cause of his unrest.

'If you really love the Grasslands so much,' she said to him one day, 'why didn't you stay there? Why did you come back?'

'I had to,' he murmured uneasily, 'it was my duty to return.'

'No,' she said, shaking her head at him, 'it's not as simple as that. You returned because deep down you wanted to. The Grasslands is a beautiful and peaceful place, but this is your home. Like it or not, you are a part of the Greenlands, and it would have drawn you back whether Shadroth had existed or not.'

'I don't believe that,' he said doggedly. 'I felt happy amongst the Gentle Folk. I was one of them.'

'I can understand why you like to think that,' Lea said sadly, 'but it simply isn't true. Could one of the Gentle Folk have hunted Shadroth as you did? Could Shadroth ever have lodged himself in their minds as he did in yours? – for remember, you are the one who painted him. No, for better or for worse, Tal, you are a member of the Clan. You think and feel as we do; you suffer from our strengths and weaknesses. And therefore this is where you belong.'

'But Argalna left here,' he protested, 'and he is happy amongst the Gentle Folk. Why shouldn't I do the same?'

'Because you don't carry his burden of guilt,' Lea replied. 'You have never hunted the Feln or taken the charm from the cave behind the falls. Were Argalna to return, every sight and sound here in the Greenlands would be a burden of grief to him; the faces of your dead parents would confront him wherever he looked. Compared with Argalna, you are completely innocent.'

'I, innocent?' Tal said, rising hastily to his feet and moving a short distance down the hillside. 'You don't know what you're saying.'

Lea remained silent for several minutes, allowing him to regain his composure.

'It's the Feln, isn't it?' she said at last, speaking softly.

He whirled around, his eyes brimming with tears.

'Of course it's the Feln!' he almost shouted.

'But how do you know she's dead?' Lea asked.

'Because I left her lying helpless on the bank beside the pool, with Shadroth only a few paces away. I ran off and left her when she was unable to defend herself!'

'What else could you have done?' Lea argued. 'You had to get the charm to the cave. You know that.'

'Kulok also knew that,' Tal countered, 'but it didn't stop him coming to my rescue when I was trapped up there on the ledge.'

'But that was different, Tal.'

'No, not different! If Kulok had run off and left me, I would have been killed and thrown over the edge of the cliff – much as the Feln was killed and her body cast into the river.'

He half turned away, wiping his arm across his eyes.

'That is one possible explanation,' Lea said.

'Is there any other?' he replied shortly.

'Yes,' Lea said quietly. 'It's quite possible that your actions saved the Feln. You might have distracted Shadroth and given her time to crawl away into the trees.'

Tal glanced up sharply, a questioning look in his eyes.

'Then why hasn't she reappeared?' he asked.

'The Feln is a wild creature, Tal,' Lea explained. 'Her place is not with us. She has her own kind, her own instincts to obey. Isn't that why we fought Shadroth – so that she and every other creature in the Greenlands could be free?'

Tal came forward and crouched before Lea.

'What are you saying?' he asked quietly.

Lea stood up and beckoned for him to follow.

'It's probably better if I show you,' she said.

Together, they entered the Greenlands and walked quickly along one of the paths. After a few minutes, Lea pointed over to the right and indicated that Tal should go first. As there was no path in that direction, he had to force his way through the heavy growth of bushes and vines. It was slow, difficult work, and he was about to ask where they were going when suddenly he realized that this had all happened to him once before – except that on the first occasion it had taken place in a dream – the dream he had had in the cave the night before they had returned to the Slopes. Yes, that was it. He had been walking through exactly this part of the Greenlands. Ahead of him, there had been a clearing; and he had known that if he could only reach it, everything would be as it had been before the coming of Shadroth.

He looked up and saw the clearing: a broad band of sunlight only about ten paces from where he now stood. Pushing his way through the tangle of bushes, he came to that last green branch which hung heavily across his path. He reached out to grasp it, and on this occasion nobody shook him awake. Pulling it aside, he stepped forward into the clearing – in time to see a fluffy ball of gold disappear behind a clump of grass. It was not the Feln herself, but a small Feln cub; followed a second later by another – the two tiny creatures wrestling playfully together in the sunlight.

Tal walked quietly over and was about to pick them up when a warning growl made him draw back. This time it was the Feln: he recognized her by the ridge of scar across her neck. Again she growled protectively and Tal thought for a moment that she had forgotten him. But he should not have doubted her. After only the briefest of hesitations, she came up and nuzzled him with her warm gentle mouth. As he reached up to stroke her head, Lea, from behind him, said softly:

'Do you still want to leave the Greenlands, Tal?'

Before he could reply, one of the tiny cubs leaped inquisitively into his lap and licked his arm with its small, rough tongue. It was, as he recognized immediately, a better answer than any he could have given. Laughing with pleasure, he glanced across at Lea's smiling face. And he knew then that although a part of him would always hanker for the peaceful life of the Grasslands, it was here that he truly belonged.